Courtney Crumrin Tales

A Portrait of the Warlock as a young man

By
Ted Naifeh

Design by
Ted Naifeh & Keith Wood

Edited by
Joe Nozemack & James Lucas Jones

publisher
Joe Nozemack

managing editor
Randal C. Jarrell

marketing and sales director
Maryanne Snell

ONI PRESS, INC.
1305 SE Martin Luther King Jr. Blvd.
Suite A
Portland, OR 97214
USA

www.onipress.com

www.tednaifeh.com

First edition: July 2005
ISBN 1-932664-32-7

1 3 5 7 9 10 8 6 4 2
PRINTED IN CANADA.

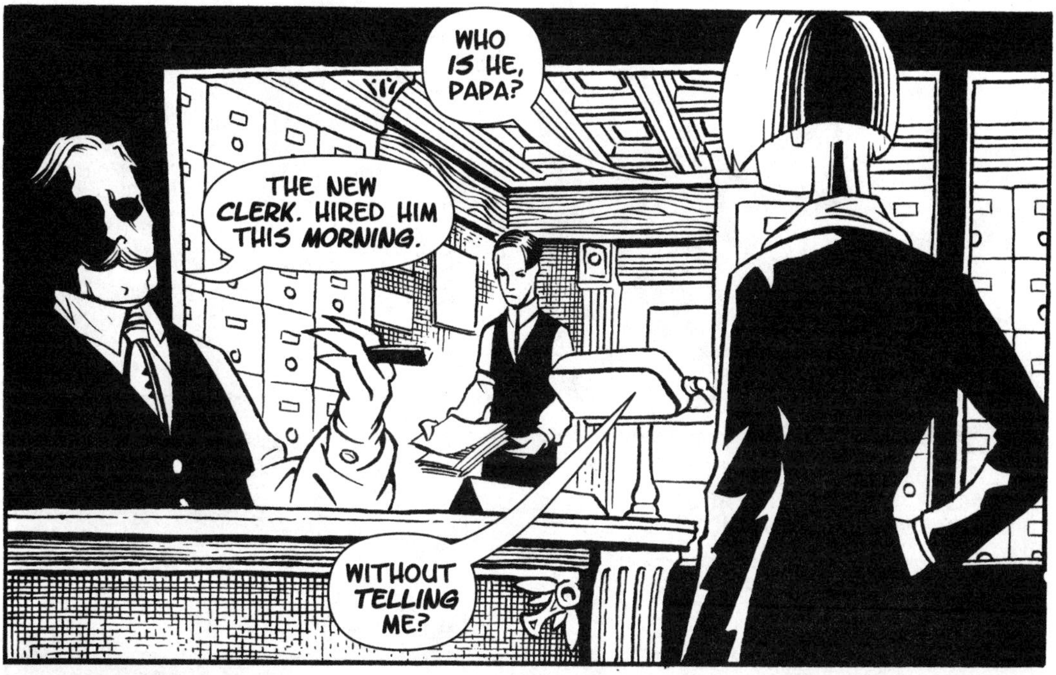
WHO IS HE, PAPA?
THE NEW CLERK. HIRED HIM THIS MORNING.
WITHOUT TELLING ME?

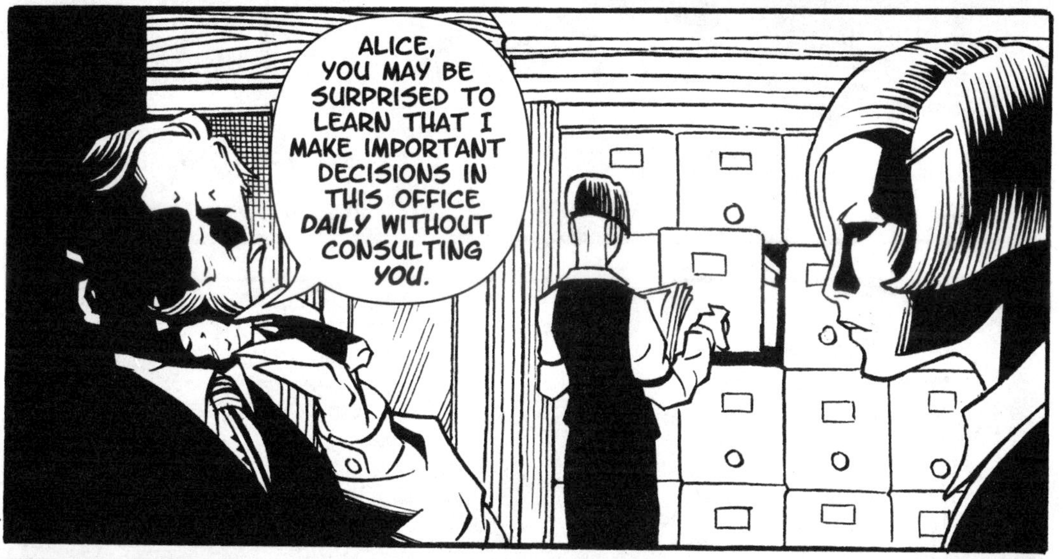
ALICE, YOU MAY BE SURPRISED TO LEARN THAT I MAKE IMPORTANT DECISIONS IN THIS OFFICE DAILY WITHOUT CONSULTING YOU.

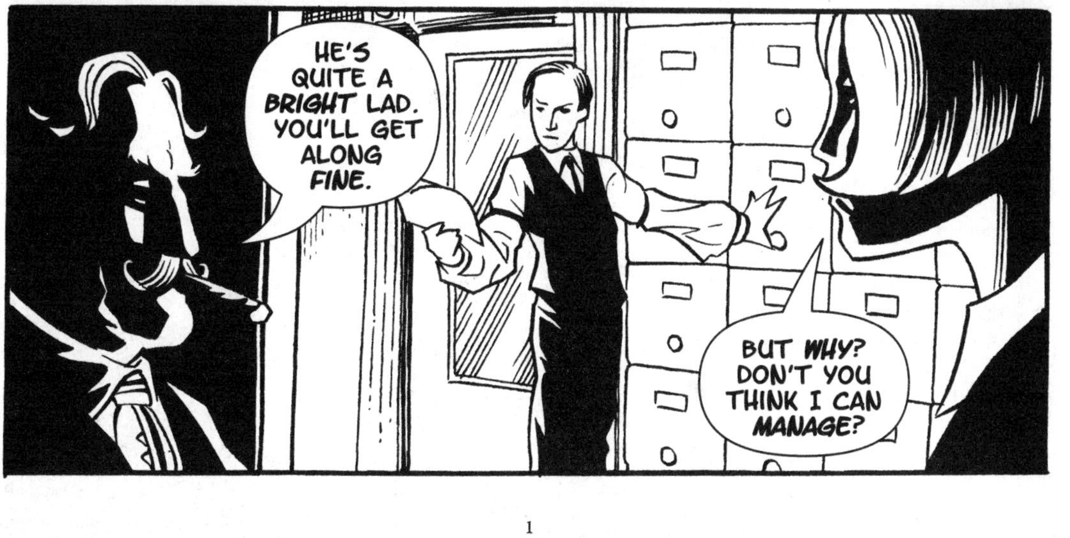
HE'S QUITE A BRIGHT LAD. YOU'LL GET ALONG FINE.
BUT WHY? DON'T YOU THINK I CAN MANAGE?

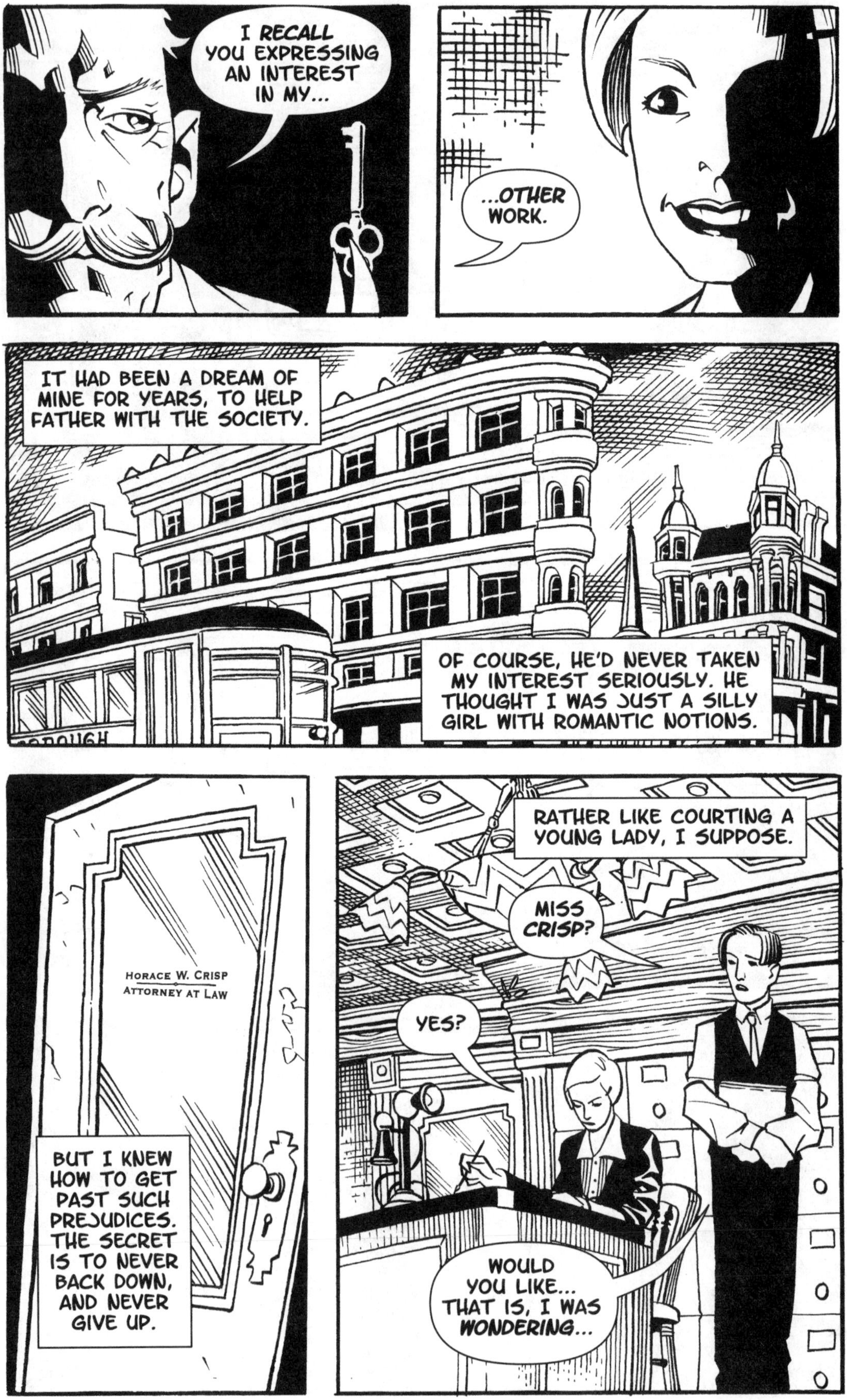
I RECALL YOU EXPRESSING AN INTEREST IN MY...
...OTHER WORK.
IT HAD BEEN A DREAM OF MINE FOR YEARS, TO HELP FATHER WITH THE SOCIETY.
OF COURSE, HE'D NEVER TAKEN MY INTEREST SERIOUSLY. HE THOUGHT I WAS JUST A SILLY GIRL WITH ROMANTIC NOTIONS.
HORACE W. CRISP
ATTORNEY AT LAW
BUT I KNEW HOW TO GET PAST SUCH PREJUDICES. THE SECRET IS TO NEVER BACK DOWN, AND NEVER GIVE UP.
RATHER LIKE COURTING A YOUNG LADY, I SUPPOSE.
MISS CRISP?
YES?
WOULD YOU LIKE... THAT IS, I WAS WONDERING...

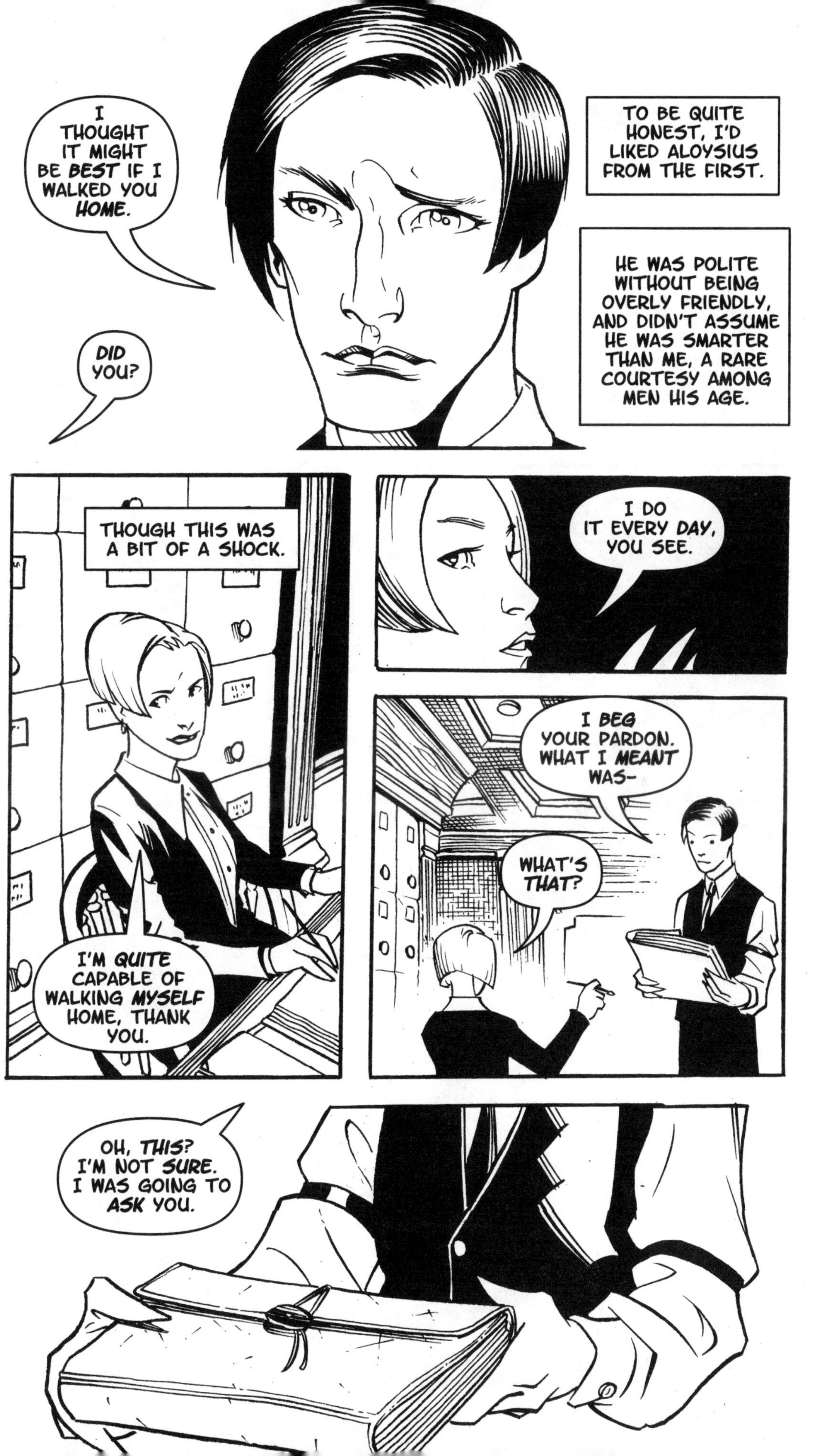

I THOUGHT IT MIGHT BE BEST IF I WALKED YOU HOME.
TO BE QUITE HONEST, I'D LIKED ALOYSIUS FROM THE FIRST.
HE WAS POLITE WITHOUT BEING OVERLY FRIENDLY, AND DIDN'T ASSUME HE WAS SMARTER THAN ME, A RARE COURTESY AMONG MEN HIS AGE.
DID YOU?
THOUGH THIS WAS A BIT OF A SHOCK.
I'M QUITE CAPABLE OF WALKING MYSELF HOME, THANK YOU.
I DO IT EVERY DAY, YOU SEE.
I BEG YOUR PARDON. WHAT I MEANT WAS-
WHAT'S THAT?
OH, THIS? I'M NOT SURE. I WAS GOING TO ASK YOU.

MULTIPLE VANISHINGS

THE SORCERER OF GREEN STREET
a first hand account

1912 SIGHTINGS OF THE HILLSBOROUGH BOGIE

THIS WAS MISFILED UNDER HILLSBOROUGH *PROPERTY* DISPUTES.

NEEDLESS TO SAY, I WAS RATHER TAKEN ABACK BY IT.

UNTIL RECENTLY, I'D SEEN ONLY GLIMPSES OF FATHER'S REAL WORK. I COULDN'T HELP BUT LINGER OVER THEM A MOMENT.

IS THIS SOME SORT OF *HOBBY* OF MR. CRISP'S? COLLECTING HUMBUG STORIES?

IT'S NONE OF YOUR *CONCERN.*

I MEANT NO OFFENCE.

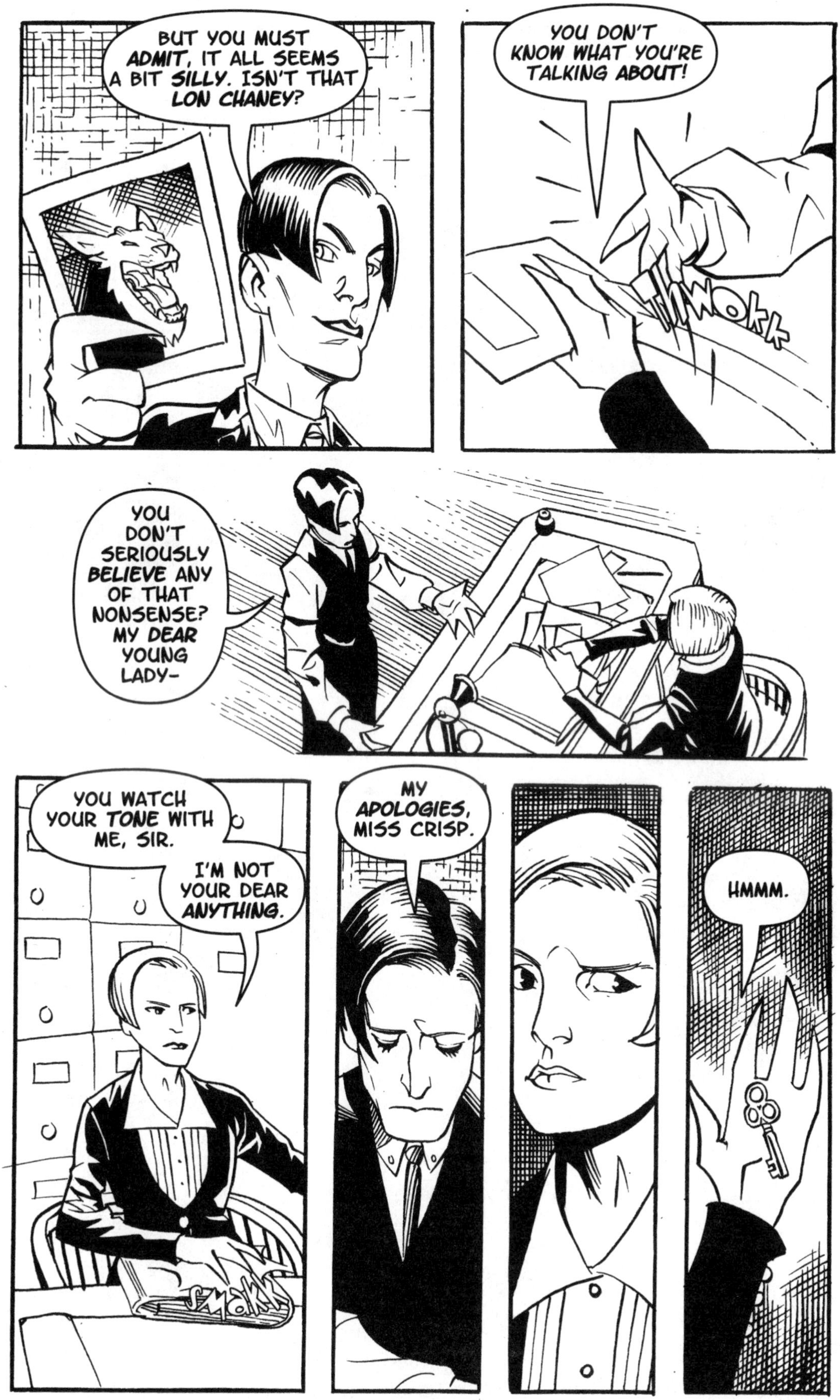
BUT YOU MUST ADMIT, IT ALL SEEMS A BIT SILLY. ISN'T THAT LON CHANEY?
YOU DON'T KNOW WHAT YOU'RE TALKING ABOUT!
THWOKK
YOU DON'T SERIOUSLY BELIEVE ANY OF THAT NONSENSE? MY DEAR YOUNG LADY-
YOU WATCH YOUR TONE WITH ME, SIR.
I'M NOT YOUR DEAR ANYTHING.
SMAKK
MY APOLOGIES, MISS CRISP.
HMMM.

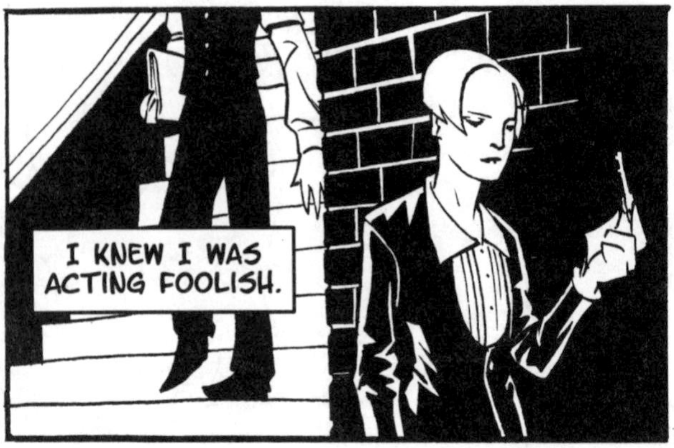
I KNEW I WAS ACTING FOOLISH.

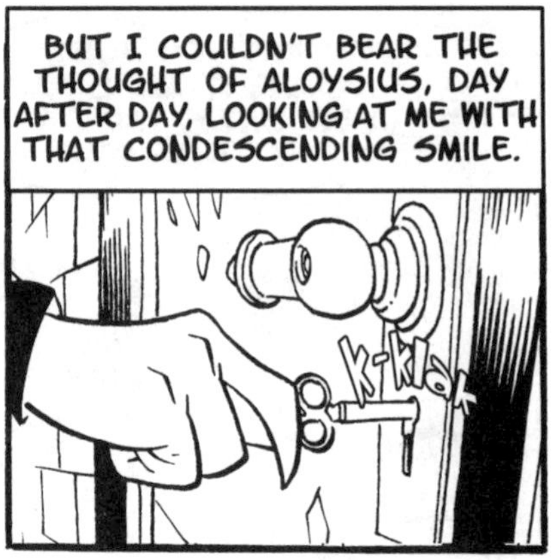
BUT I COULDN'T BEAR THE THOUGHT OF ALOYSIUS, DAY AFTER DAY, LOOKING AT ME WITH THAT CONDESCENDING SMILE.
K-KLAK

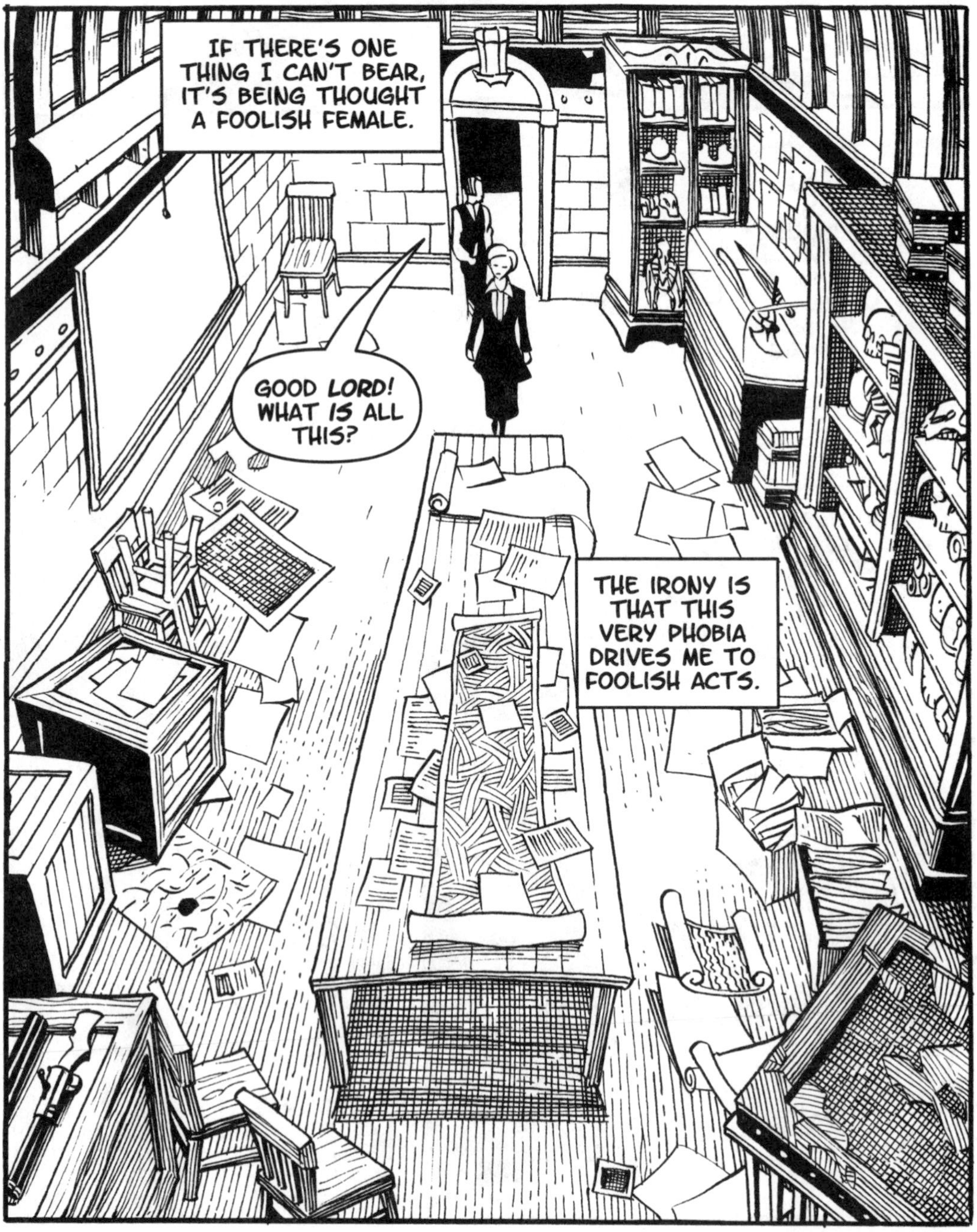
IF THERE'S ONE THING I CAN'T BEAR, IT'S BEING THOUGHT A FOOLISH FEMALE.
GOOD LORD! WHAT IS ALL THIS?
THE IRONY IS THAT THIS VERY PHOBIA DRIVES ME TO FOOLISH ACTS.

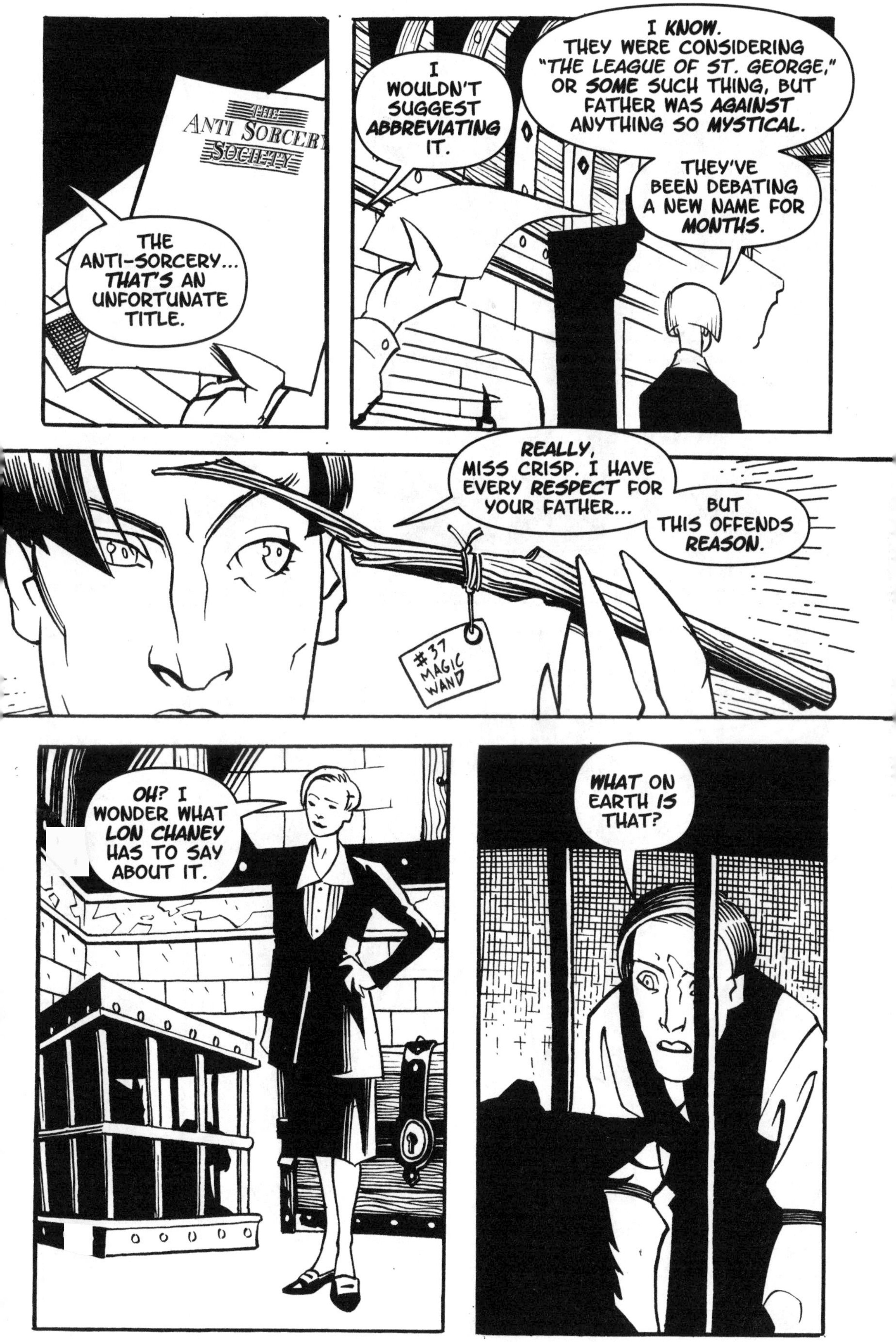
THE ANTI SORCERY SOCIETY
THE ANTI-SORCERY... THAT'S AN UNFORTUNATE TITLE.
I WOULDN'T SUGGEST ABBREVIATING IT.
I KNOW. THEY WERE CONSIDERING "THE LEAGUE OF ST. GEORGE," OR SOME SUCH THING, BUT FATHER WAS AGAINST ANYTHING SO MYSTICAL.
THEY'VE BEEN DEBATING A NEW NAME FOR MONTHS.
REALLY, MISS CRISP. I HAVE EVERY RESPECT FOR YOUR FATHER...
BUT THIS OFFENDS REASON.
#37 MAGIC WAND
OH? I WONDER WHAT LON CHANEY HAS TO SAY ABOUT IT.
WHAT ON EARTH IS THAT?

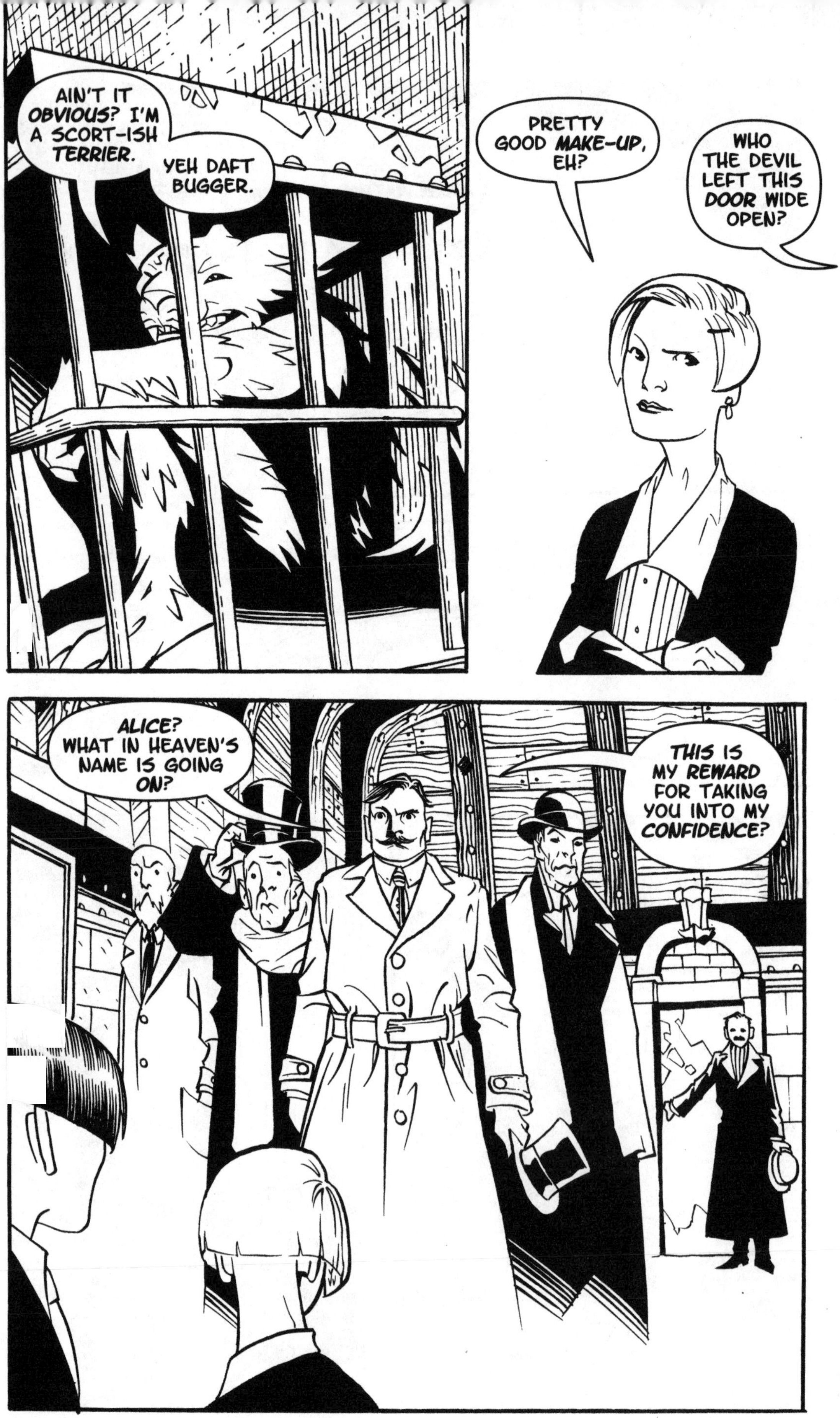
AIN'T IT OBVIOUS? I'M A SCORT-ISH TERRIER.
YEH DAFT BUGGER.
PRETTY GOOD MAKE-UP, EH?
WHO THE DEVIL LEFT THIS DOOR WIDE OPEN?
ALICE? WHAT IN HEAVEN'S NAME IS GOING ON?
THIS IS MY REWARD FOR TAKING YOU INTO MY CONFIDENCE?

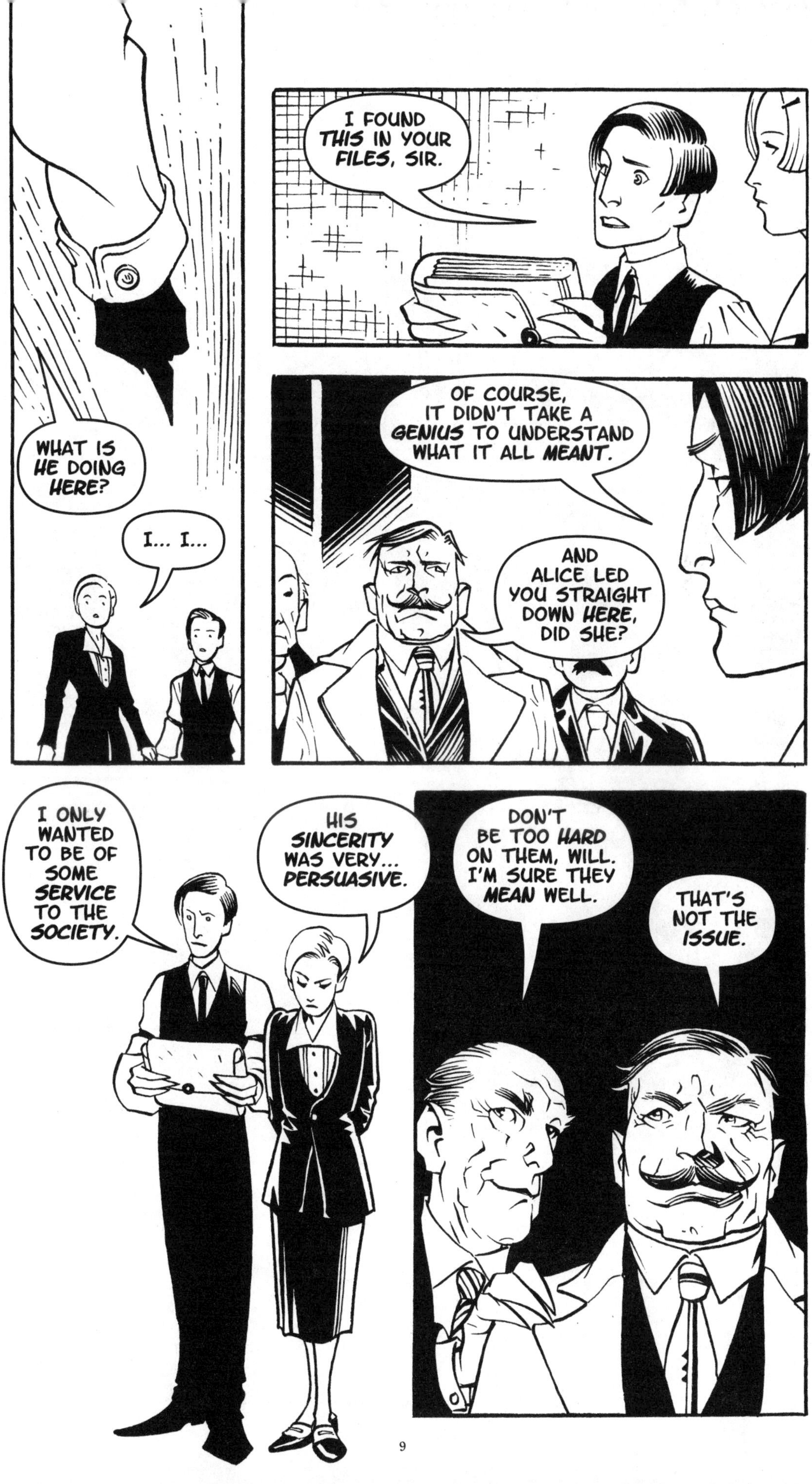
WHAT IS HE DOING HERE?
I... I...
I FOUND THIS IN YOUR FILES, SIR.
OF COURSE, IT DIDN'T TAKE A GENIUS TO UNDERSTAND WHAT IT ALL MEANT.
AND ALICE LED YOU STRAIGHT DOWN HERE, DID SHE?
I ONLY WANTED TO BE OF SOME SERVICE TO THE SOCIETY.
HIS SINCERITY WAS VERY... PERSUASIVE.
DON'T BE TOO HARD ON THEM, WILL. I'M SURE THEY MEAN WELL.
THAT'S NOT THE ISSUE.

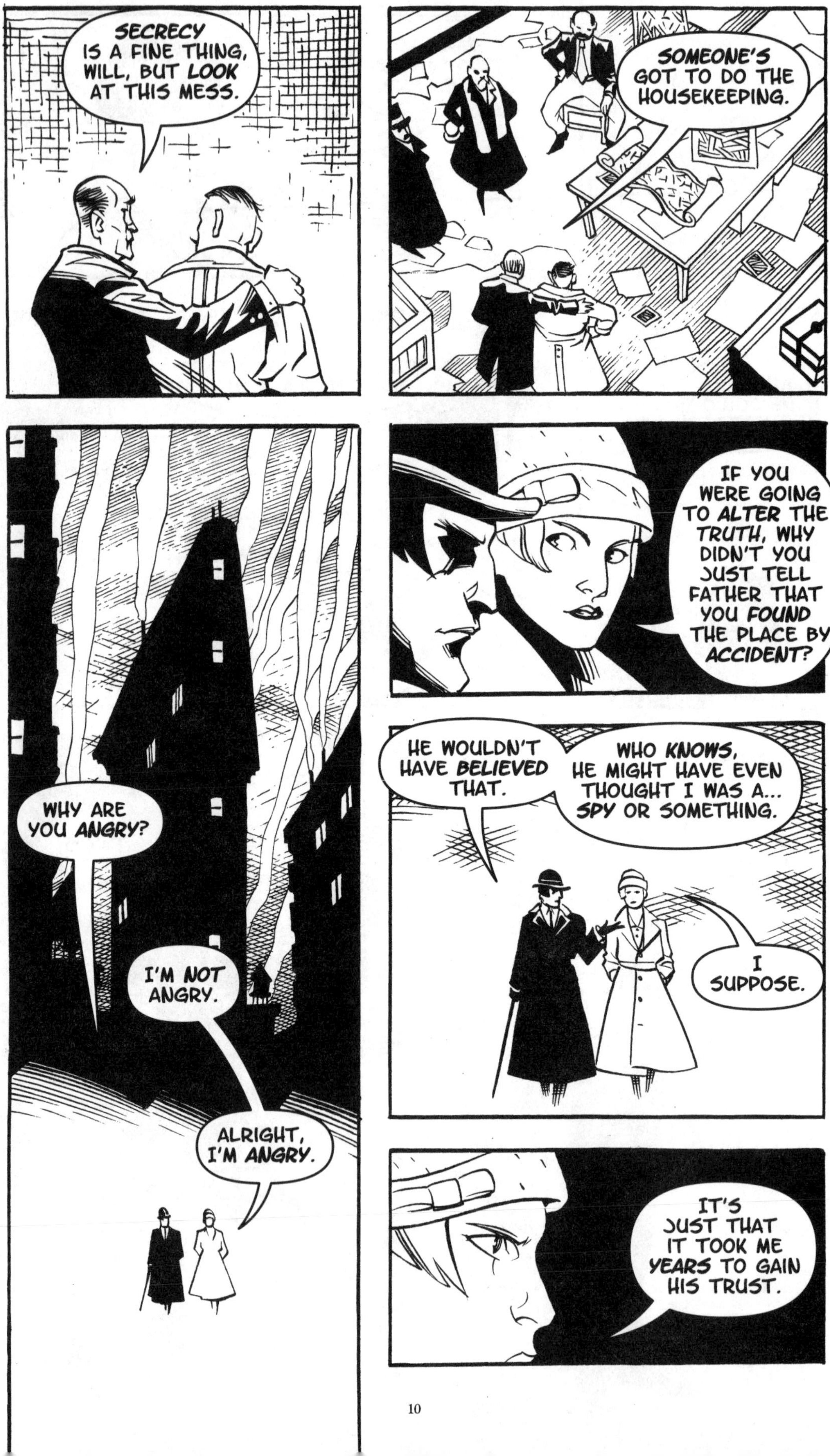
SECRECY IS A FINE THING, WILL, BUT LOOK AT THIS MESS.
SOMEONE'S GOT TO DO THE HOUSEKEEPING.
WHY ARE YOU ANGRY?
I'M NOT ANGRY.
ALRIGHT, I'M ANGRY.
IF YOU WERE GOING TO ALTER THE TRUTH, WHY DIDN'T YOU JUST TELL FATHER THAT YOU FOUND THE PLACE BY ACCIDENT?
HE WOULDN'T HAVE BELIEVED THAT.
WHO KNOWS, HE MIGHT HAVE EVEN THOUGHT I WAS A... SPY OR SOMETHING.
I SUPPOSE.
IT'S JUST THAT IT TOOK ME YEARS TO GAIN HIS TRUST.

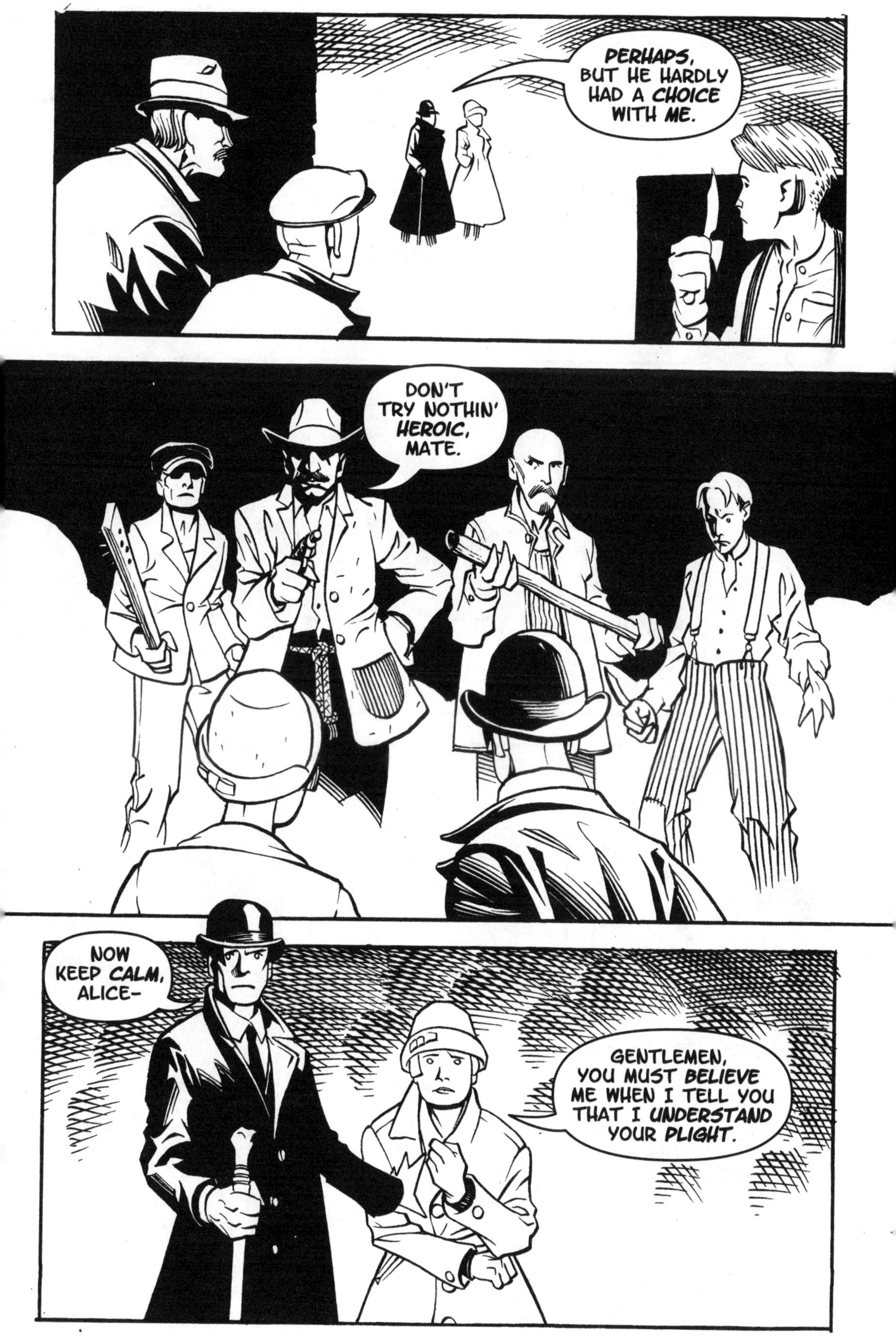
PERHAPS, BUT HE HARDLY HAD A CHOICE WITH ME.
DON'T TRY NOTHIN' HEROIC, MATE.
NOW KEEP CALM, ALICE-
GENTLEMEN, YOU MUST BELIEVE ME WHEN I TELL YOU THAT I UNDERSTAND YOUR PLIGHT.

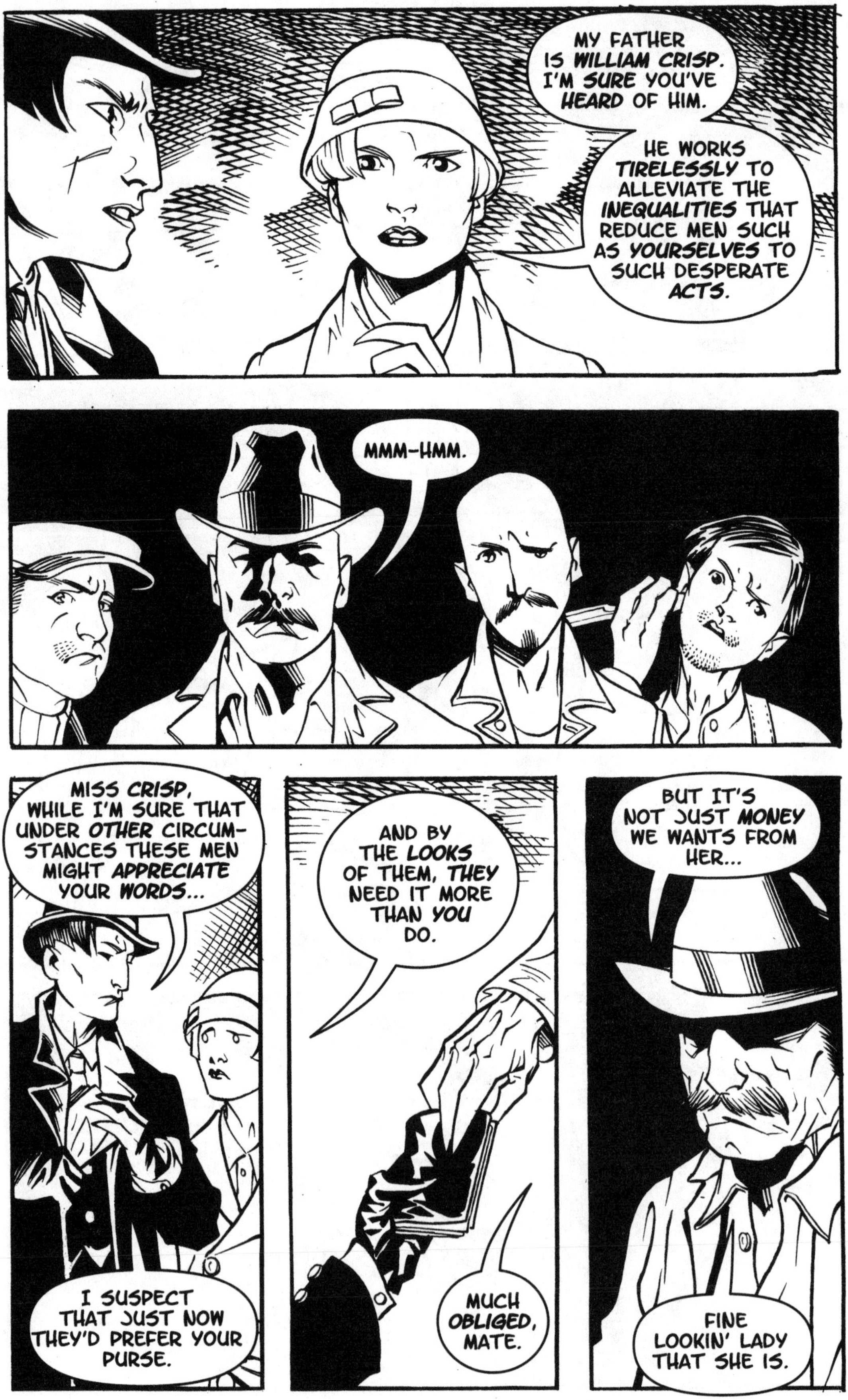
MY FATHER IS WILLIAM CRISP. I'M SURE YOU'VE HEARD OF HIM.
HE WORKS TIRELESSLY TO ALLEVIATE THE INEQUALITIES THAT REDUCE MEN SUCH AS YOURSELVES TO SUCH DESPERATE ACTS.
MMM-HMM.
MISS CRISP, WHILE I'M SURE THAT UNDER OTHER CIRCUMSTANCES THESE MEN MIGHT APPRECIATE YOUR WORDS...
I SUSPECT THAT JUST NOW THEY'D PREFER YOUR PURSE.
AND BY THE LOOKS OF THEM, THEY NEED IT MORE THAN YOU DO.
MUCH OBLIGED, MATE.
BUT IT'S NOT JUST MONEY WE WANTS FROM HER...
FINE LOOKIN' LADY THAT SHE IS.

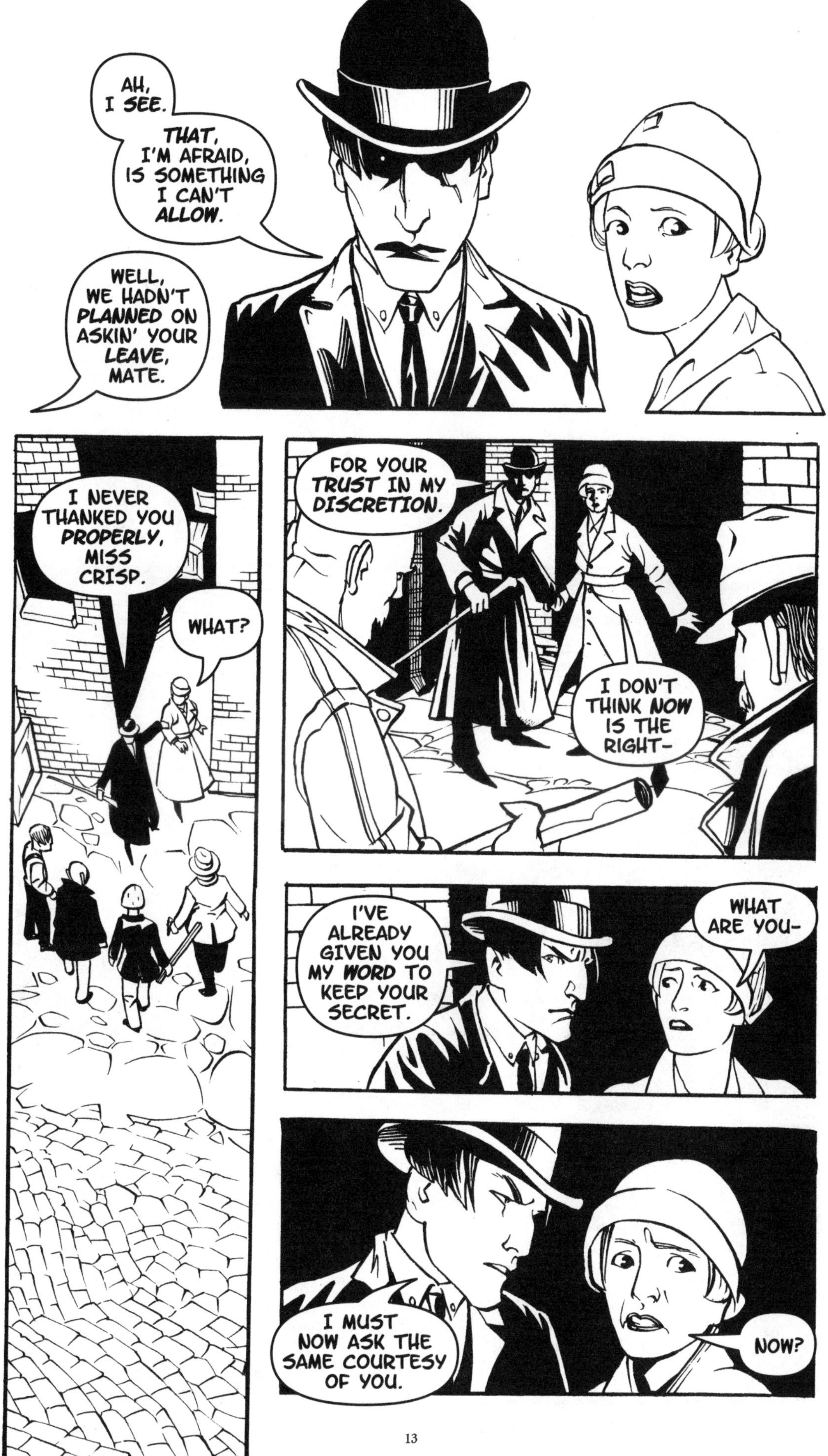
AH, I SEE.
THAT, I'M AFRAID, IS SOMETHING I CAN'T ALLOW.
WELL, WE HADN'T PLANNED ON ASKIN' YOUR LEAVE, MATE.
I NEVER THANKED YOU PROPERLY, MISS CRISP.
WHAT?
FOR YOUR TRUST IN MY DISCRETION.
I DON'T THINK NOW IS THE RIGHT-
I'VE ALREADY GIVEN YOU MY WORD TO KEEP YOUR SECRET.
WHAT ARE YOU-
I MUST NOW ASK THE SAME COURTESY OF YOU.
NOW?

YES.

ALRIGHT, BUT WHAT—

YOU SEE, THE FACT OF THE MATTER IS...

I AM A SORCERER MYSELF.

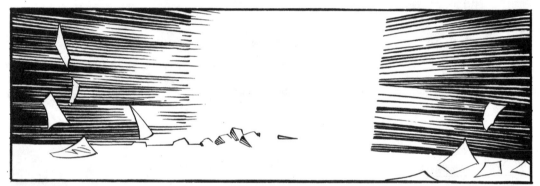

WHAT THE BLEEDIN' 'ELL WAS THAT?

I DON'T KNOW. WHAT HAPPENED TO ME CLOTHES?

LEAST YOU STILL GOT YOUR HAT. BETTER PUT IT TO USE THERE, LAD.

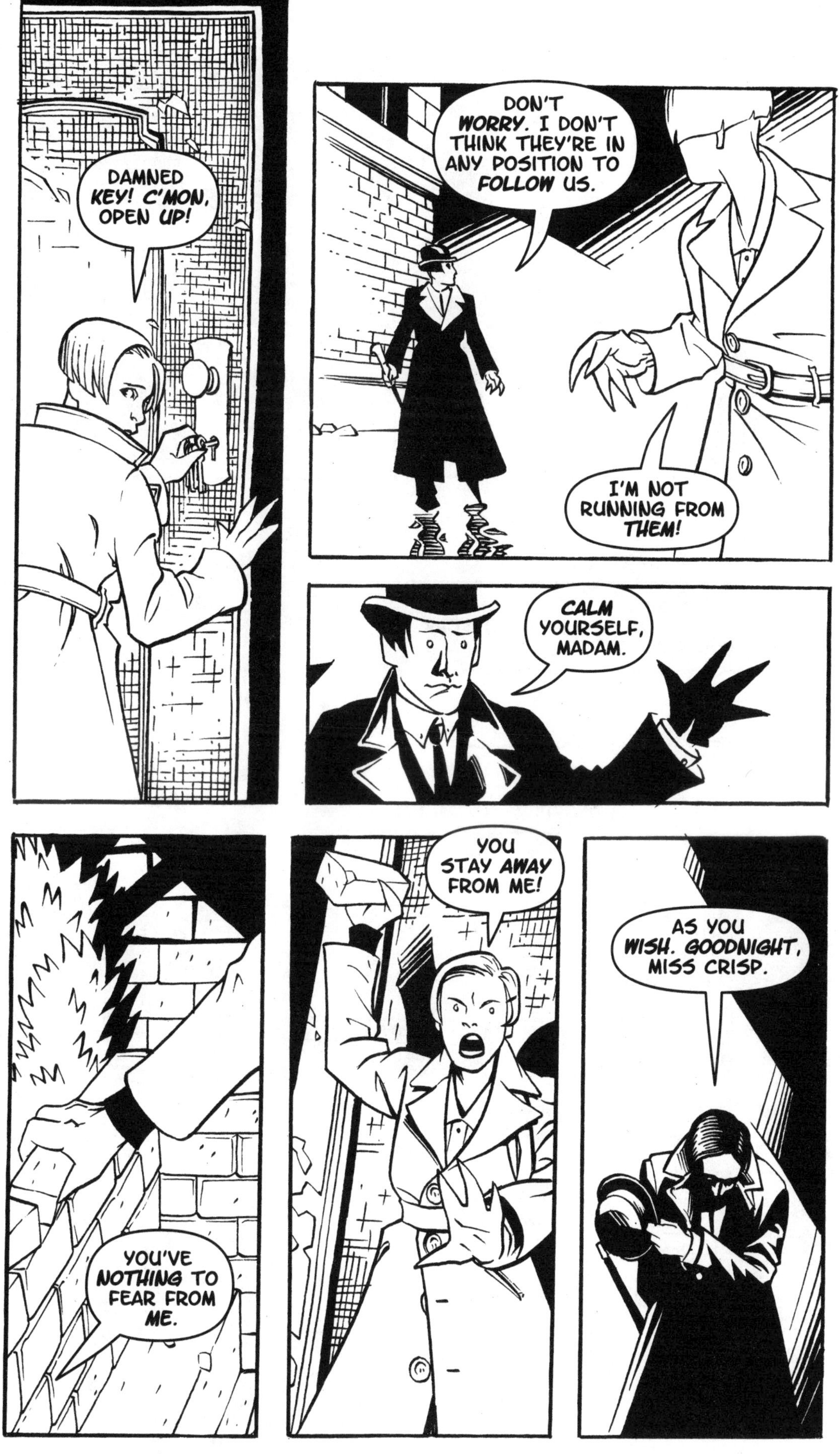
DAMNED KEY! C'MON, OPEN UP!
DON'T WORRY. I DON'T THINK THEY'RE IN ANY POSITION TO FOLLOW US.
I'M NOT RUNNING FROM THEM!
CALM YOURSELF, MADAM.
YOU'VE NOTHING TO FEAR FROM ME.
YOU STAY AWAY FROM ME!
AS YOU WISH. GOODNIGHT, MISS CRISP.

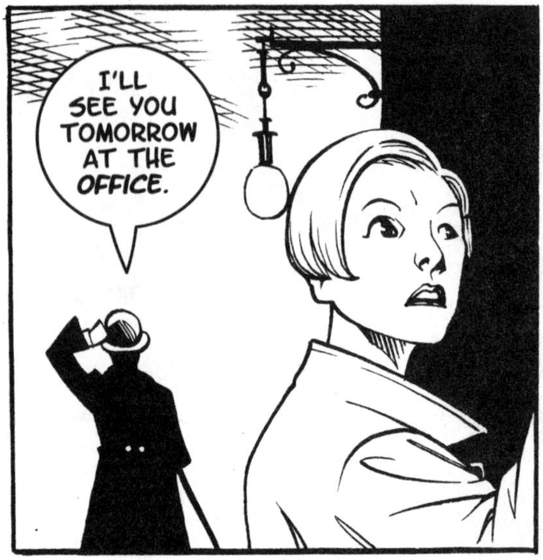
I'LL SEE YOU TOMORROW AT THE OFFICE.

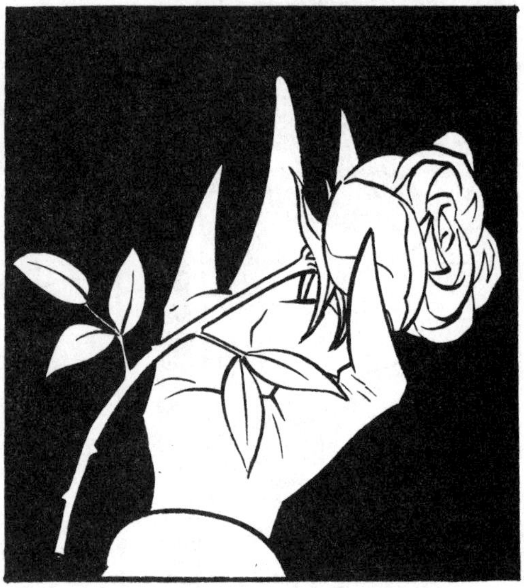

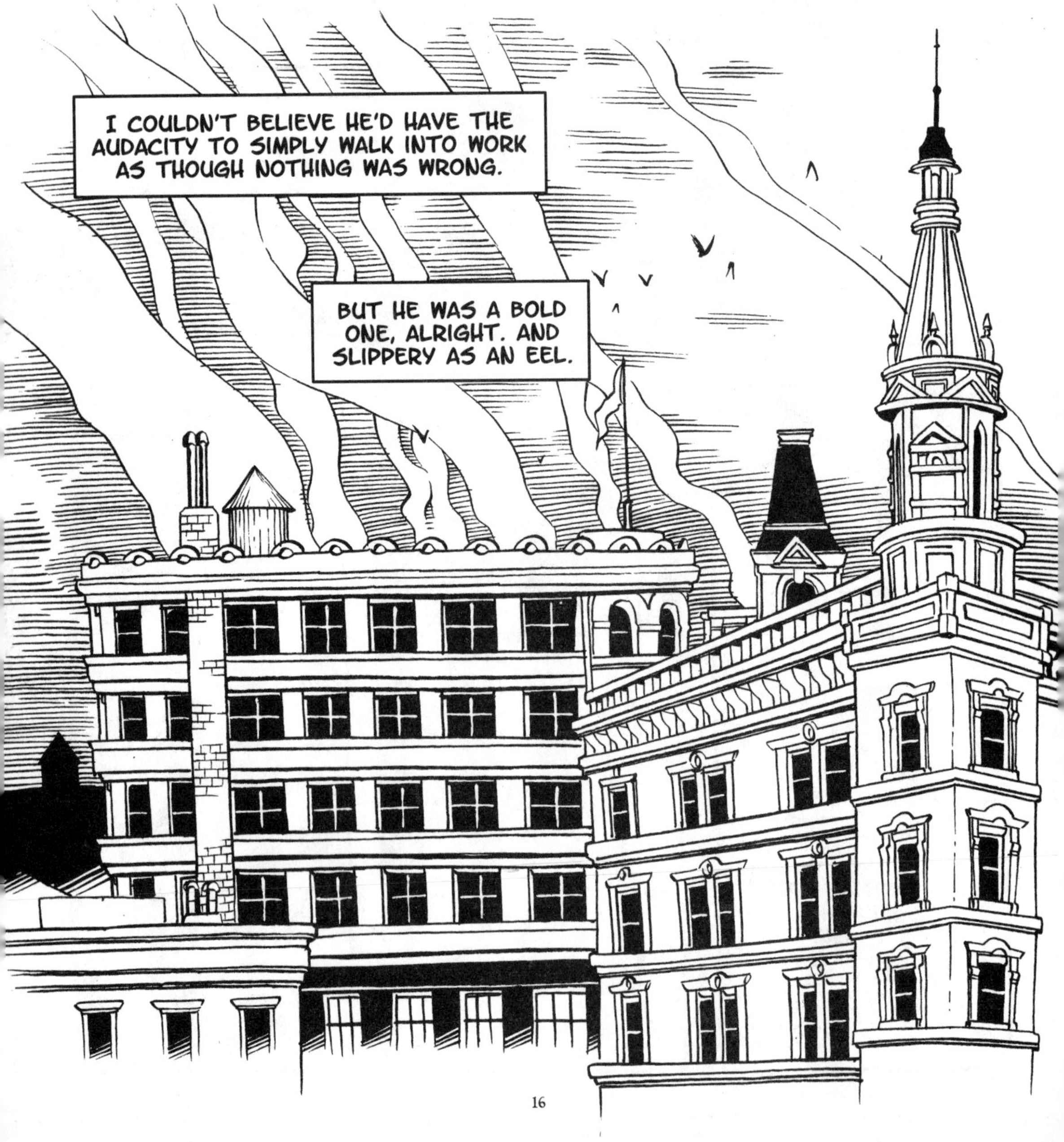
I COULDN'T BELIEVE HE'D HAVE THE AUDACITY TO SIMPLY WALK INTO WORK AS THOUGH NOTHING WAS WRONG.
BUT HE WAS A BOLD ONE, ALRIGHT. AND SLIPPERY AS AN EEL.

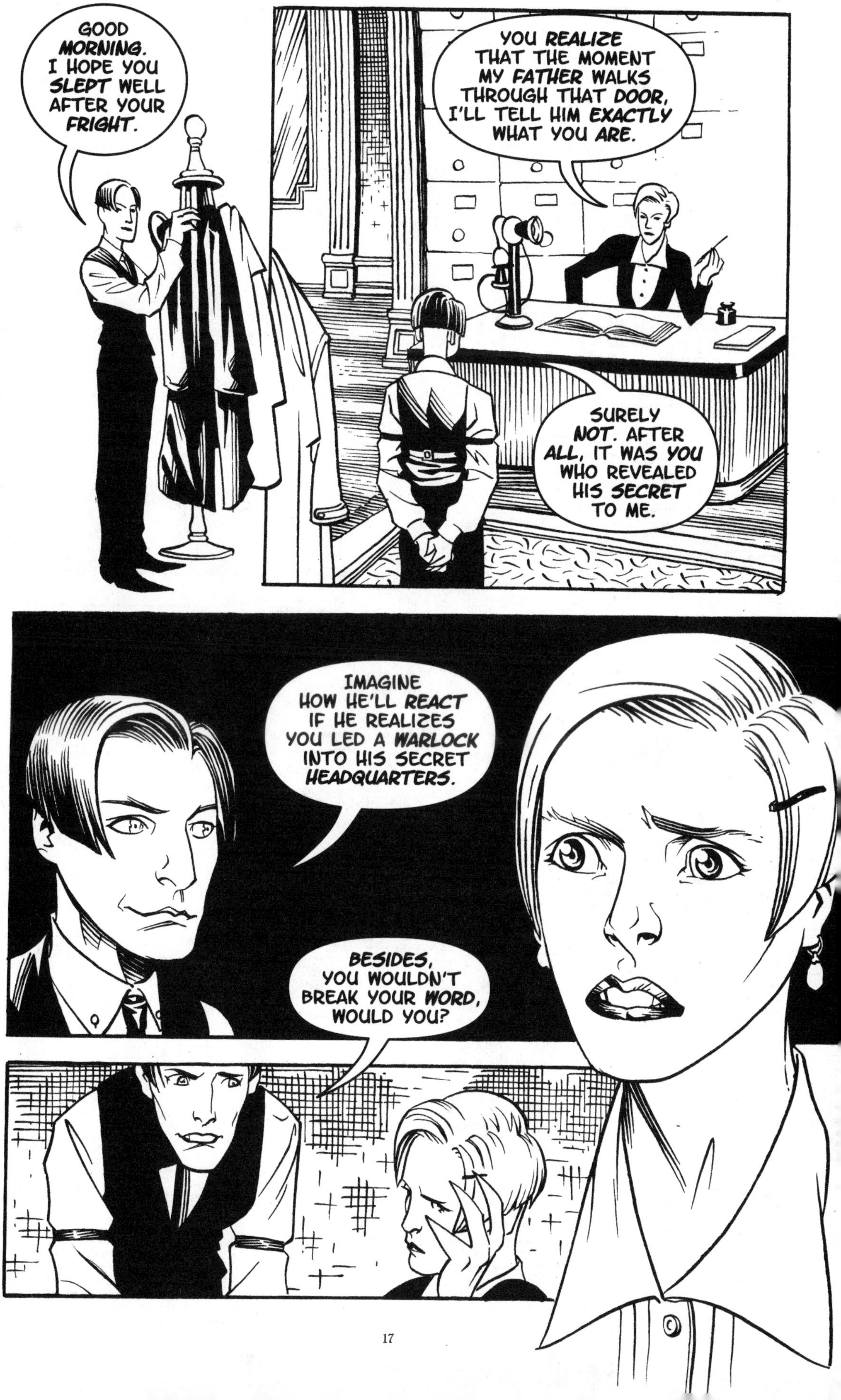
GOOD MORNING. I HOPE YOU SLEPT WELL AFTER YOUR FRIGHT.
YOU REALIZE THAT THE MOMENT MY FATHER WALKS THROUGH THAT DOOR, I'LL TELL HIM EXACTLY WHAT YOU ARE.
SURELY NOT. AFTER ALL, IT WAS YOU WHO REVEALED HIS SECRET TO ME.
IMAGINE HOW HE'LL REACT IF HE REALIZES YOU LED A WARLOCK INTO HIS SECRET HEADQUARTERS.
BESIDES, YOU WOULDN'T BREAK YOUR WORD, WOULD YOU?

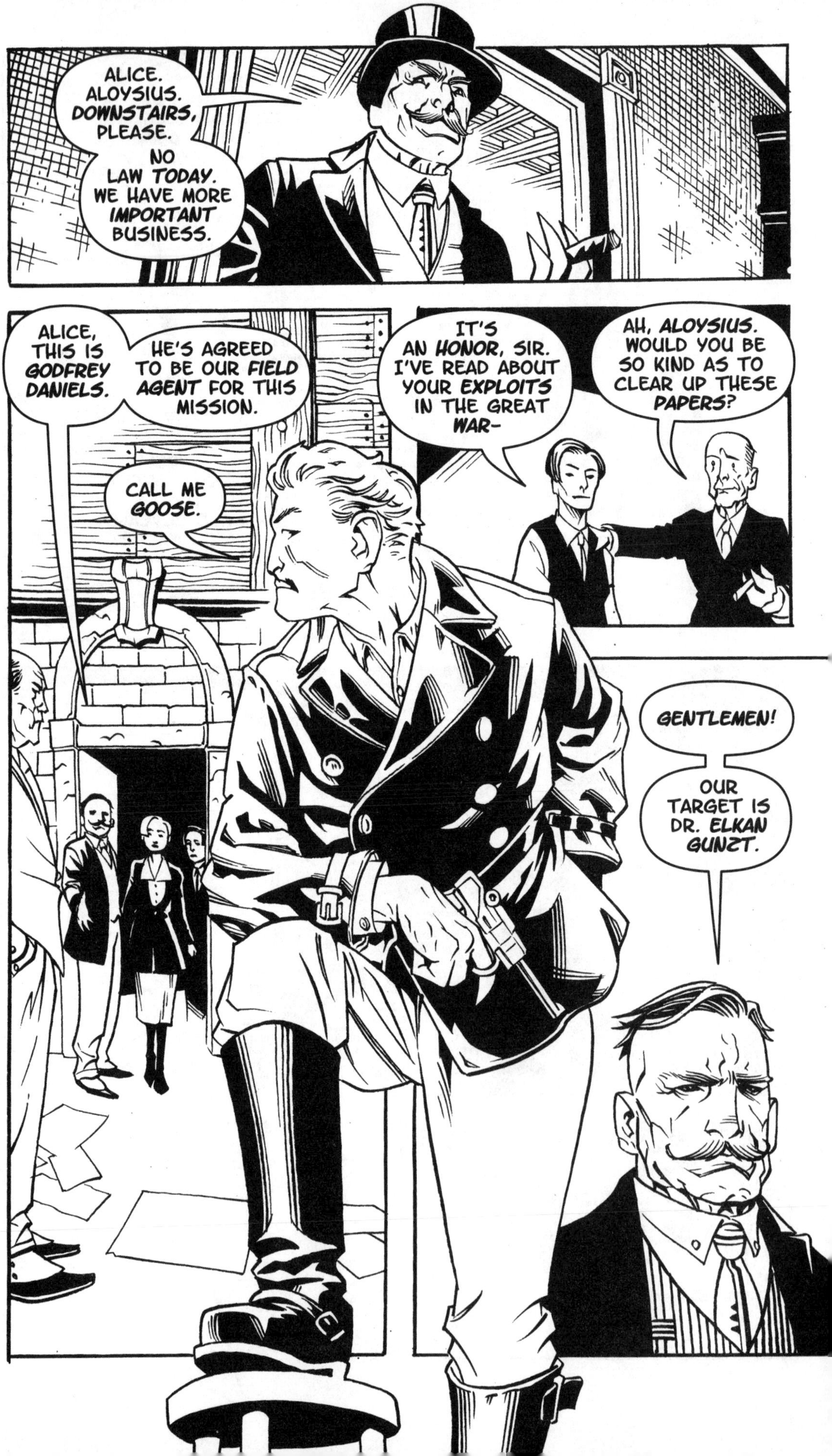
ALICE. ALOYSIUS. DOWNSTAIRS, PLEASE.
NO LAW TODAY. WE HAVE MORE IMPORTANT BUSINESS.
ALICE, THIS IS GODFREY DANIELS.
HE'S AGREED TO BE OUR FIELD AGENT FOR THIS MISSION.
CALL ME GOOSE.
IT'S AN HONOR, SIR. I'VE READ ABOUT YOUR EXPLOITS IN THE GREAT WAR-
AH, ALOYSIUS. WOULD YOU BE SO KIND AS TO CLEAR UP THESE PAPERS?
GENTLEMEN!
OUR TARGET IS DR. ELKAN GUNZT.

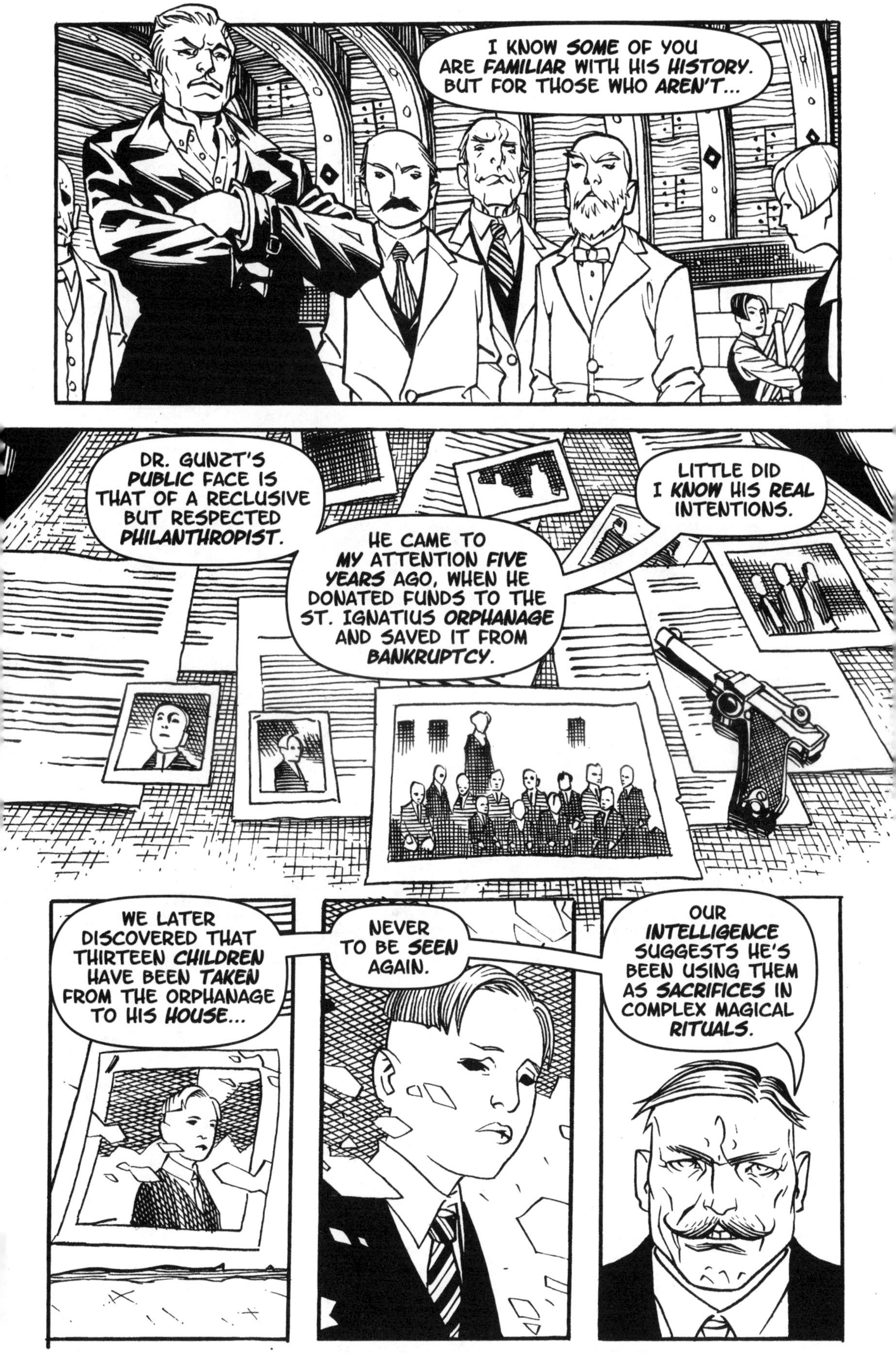
I KNOW SOME OF YOU ARE FAMILIAR WITH HIS HISTORY. BUT FOR THOSE WHO AREN'T...
DR. GUNZT'S PUBLIC FACE IS THAT OF A RECLUSIVE BUT RESPECTED PHILANTHROPIST.
HE CAME TO MY ATTENTION FIVE YEARS AGO, WHEN HE DONATED FUNDS TO THE ST. IGNATIUS ORPHANAGE AND SAVED IT FROM BANKRUPTCY.
LITTLE DID I KNOW HIS REAL INTENTIONS.
WE LATER DISCOVERED THAT THIRTEEN CHILDREN HAVE BEEN TAKEN FROM THE ORPHANAGE TO HIS HOUSE...
NEVER TO BE SEEN AGAIN.
OUR INTELLIGENCE SUGGESTS HE'S BEEN USING THEM AS SACRIFICES IN COMPLEX MAGICAL RITUALS.

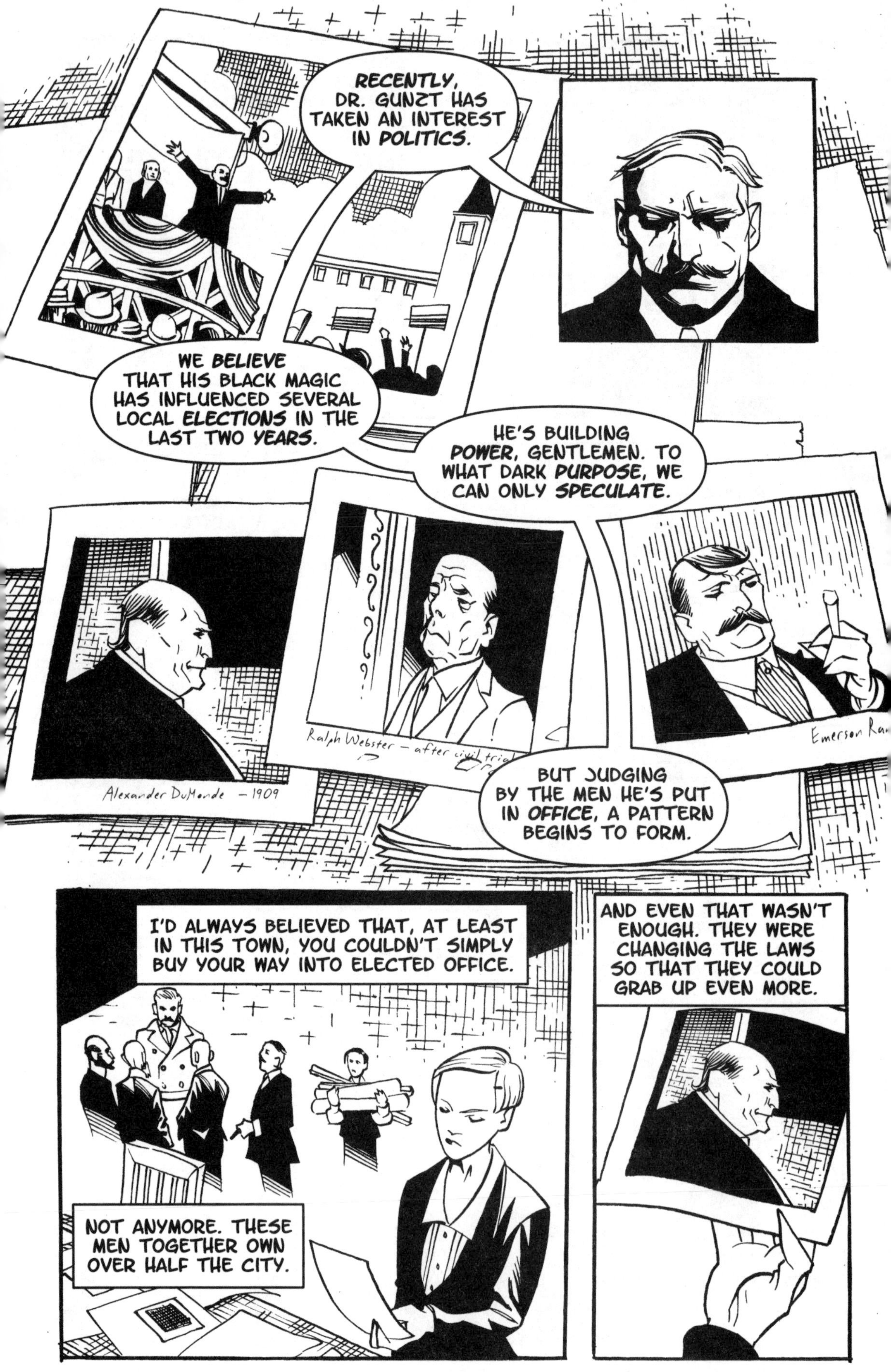

RECENTLY, DR. GUNZT HAS TAKEN AN INTEREST IN POLITICS.
WE BELIEVE THAT HIS BLACK MAGIC HAS INFLUENCED SEVERAL LOCAL ELECTIONS IN THE LAST TWO YEARS.
HE'S BUILDING POWER, GENTLEMEN. TO WHAT DARK PURPOSE, WE CAN ONLY SPECULATE.
Alexander DuMonde – 1909
Ralph Webster – after civil tri
Emerson Ra
BUT JUDGING BY THE MEN HE'S PUT IN OFFICE, A PATTERN BEGINS TO FORM.
I'D ALWAYS BELIEVED THAT, AT LEAST IN THIS TOWN, YOU COULDN'T SIMPLY BUY YOUR WAY INTO ELECTED OFFICE.
NOT ANYMORE. THESE MEN TOGETHER OWN OVER HALF THE CITY.
AND EVEN THAT WASN'T ENOUGH. THEY WERE CHANGING THE LAWS SO THAT THEY COULD GRAB UP EVEN MORE.

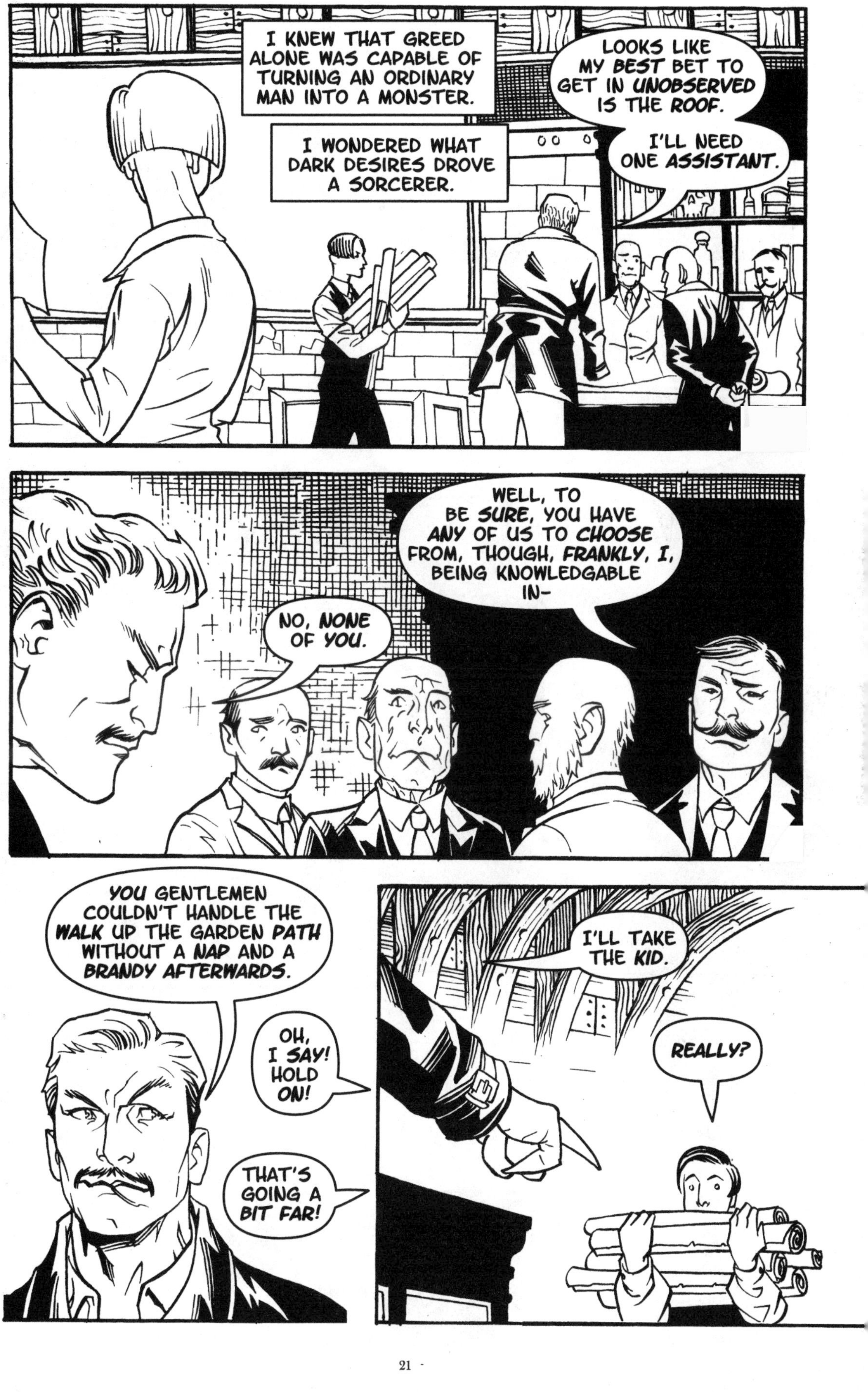
I KNEW THAT GREED ALONE WAS CAPABLE OF TURNING AN ORDINARY MAN INTO A MONSTER.
I WONDERED WHAT DARK DESIRES DROVE A SORCERER.
LOOKS LIKE MY BEST BET TO GET IN UNOBSERVED IS THE ROOF.
I'LL NEED ONE ASSISTANT.
WELL, TO BE SURE, YOU HAVE ANY OF US TO CHOOSE FROM, THOUGH, FRANKLY, I, BEING KNOWLEDGABLE IN-
NO, NONE OF YOU.
YOU GENTLEMEN COULDN'T HANDLE THE WALK UP THE GARDEN PATH WITHOUT A NAP AND A BRANDY AFTERWARDS.
OH, I SAY! HOLD ON!
THAT'S GOING A BIT FAR!
I'LL TAKE THE KID.
REALLY?

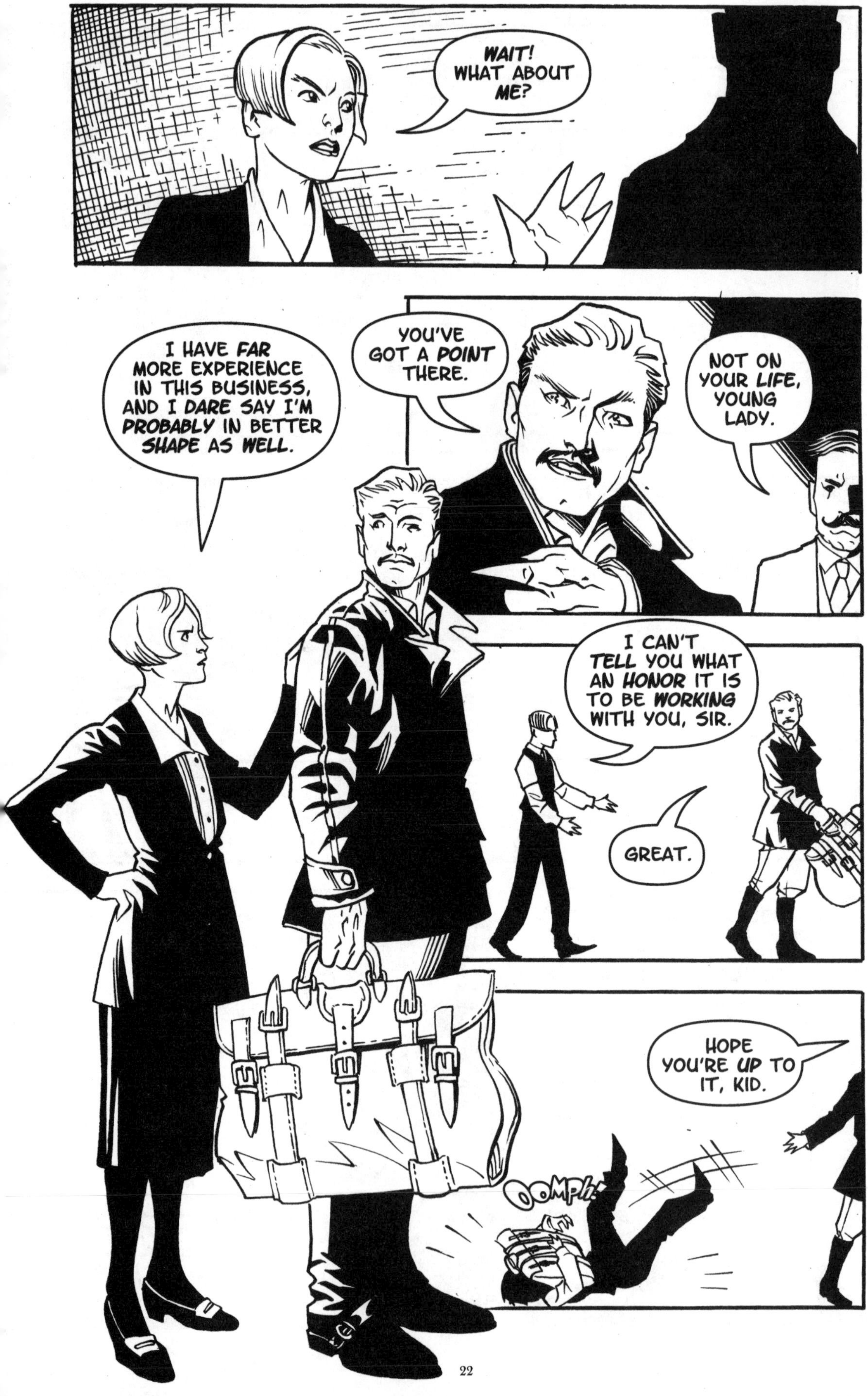
WAIT! WHAT ABOUT ME?
I HAVE FAR MORE EXPERIENCE IN THIS BUSINESS, AND I DARE SAY I'M PROBABLY IN BETTER SHAPE AS WELL.
YOU'VE GOT A POINT THERE.
NOT ON YOUR LIFE, YOUNG LADY.
I CAN'T TELL YOU WHAT AN HONOR IT IS TO BE WORKING WITH YOU, SIR.
GREAT.
HOPE YOU'RE UP TO IT, KID.
OOMPH!

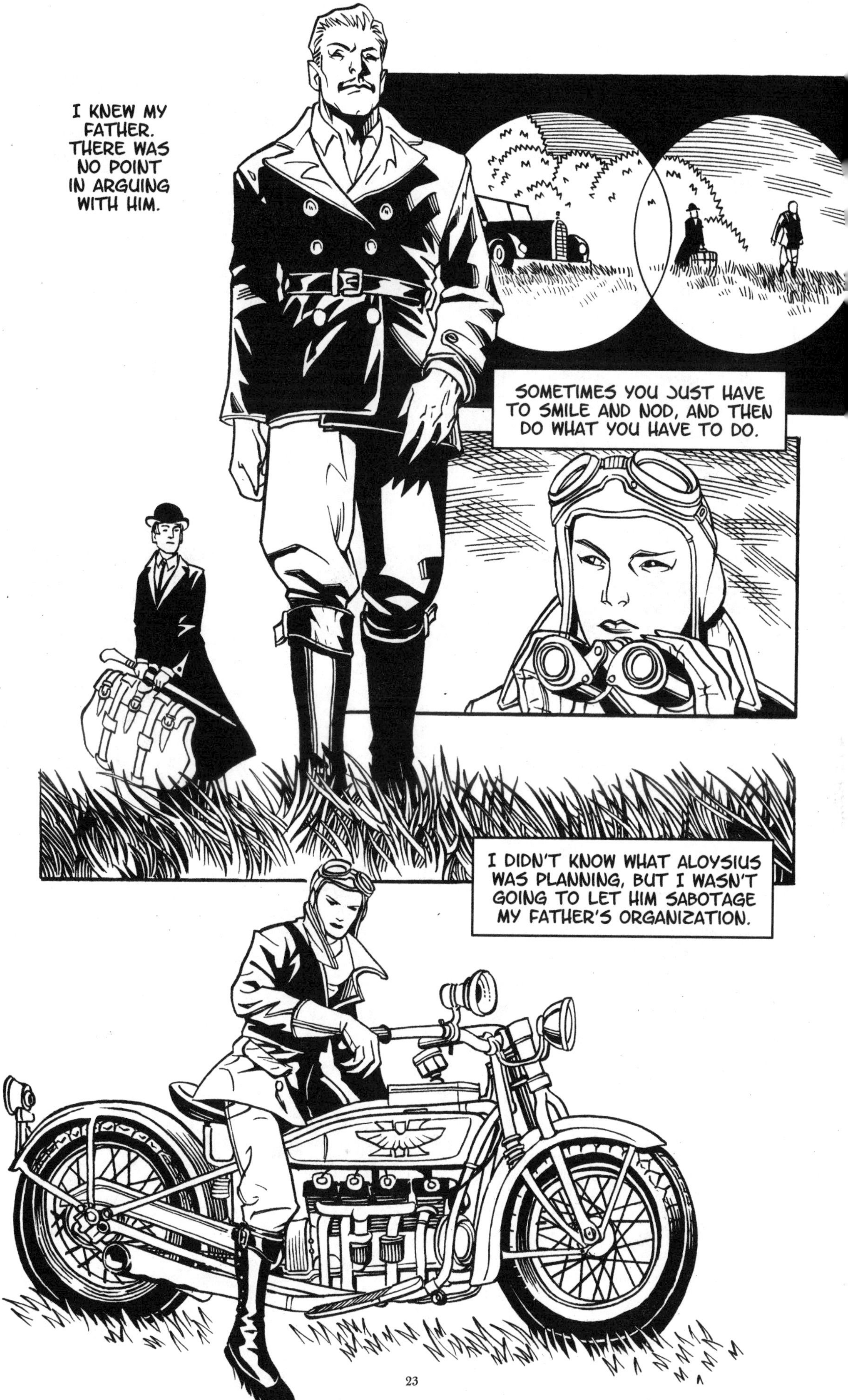
I KNEW MY FATHER. THERE WAS NO POINT IN ARGUING WITH HIM.
SOMETIMES YOU JUST HAVE TO SMILE AND NOD, AND THEN DO WHAT YOU HAVE TO DO.
I DIDN'T KNOW WHAT ALOYSIUS WAS PLANNING, BUT I WASN'T GOING TO LET HIM SABOTAGE MY FATHER'S ORGANIZATION.

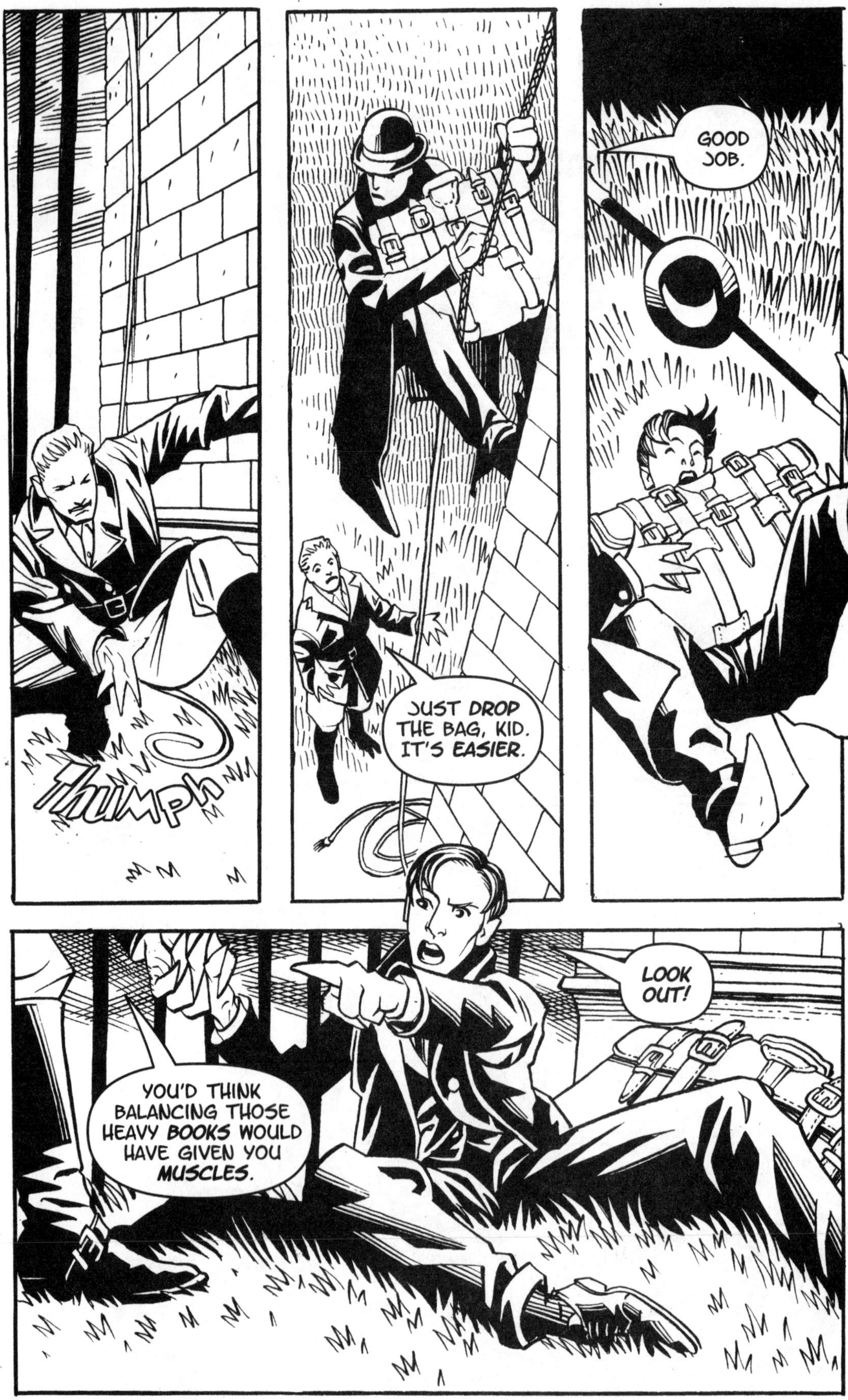
THUMPH
JUST DROP THE BAG, KID. IT'S EASIER.
GOOD JOB.
YOU'D THINK BALANCING THOSE HEAVY BOOKS WOULD HAVE GIVEN YOU MUSCLES.
LOOK OUT!

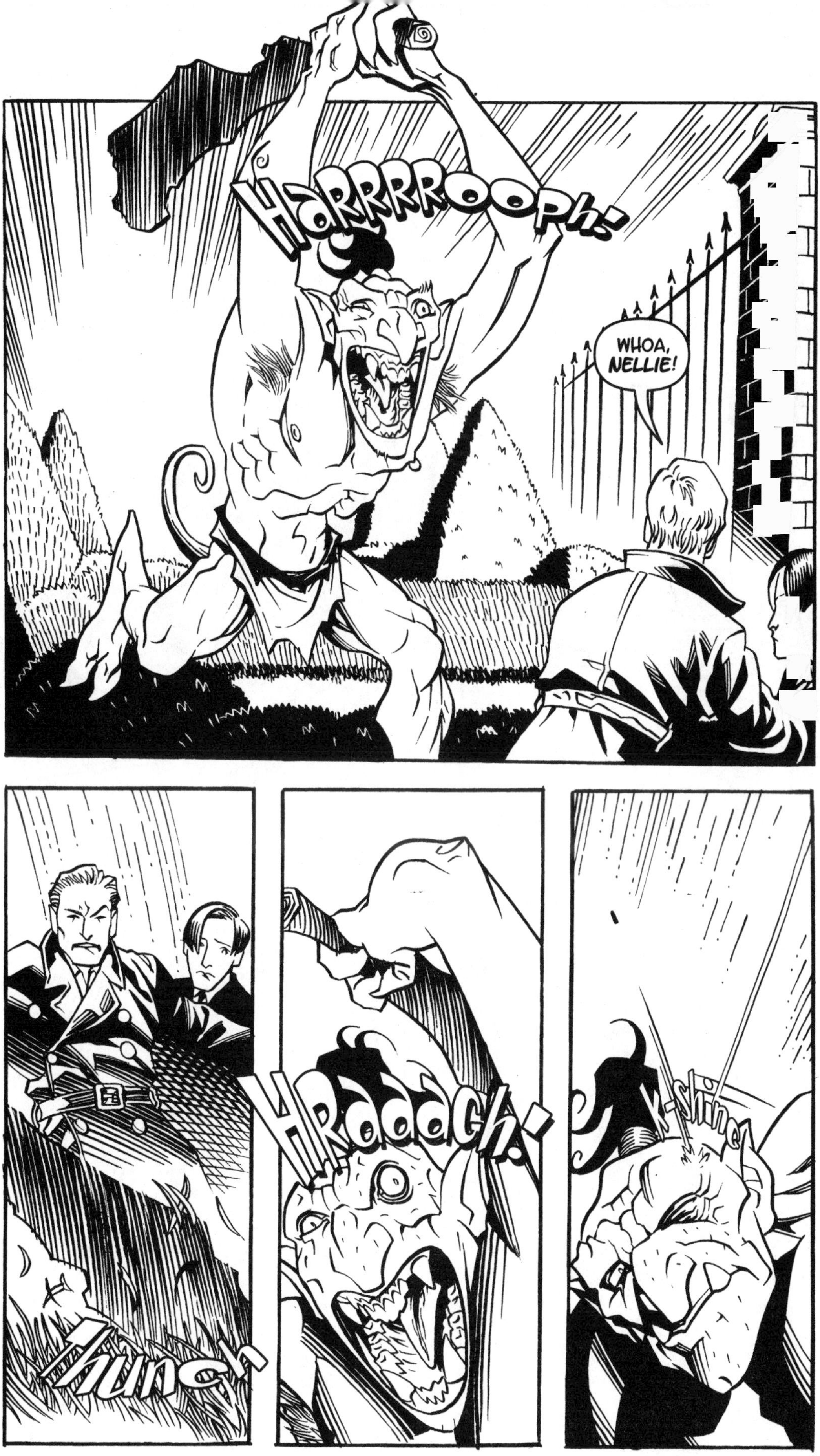
HaRRRROOPh!
WHOA, NELLIE!
thunch
HRaaaCh!
k-shine

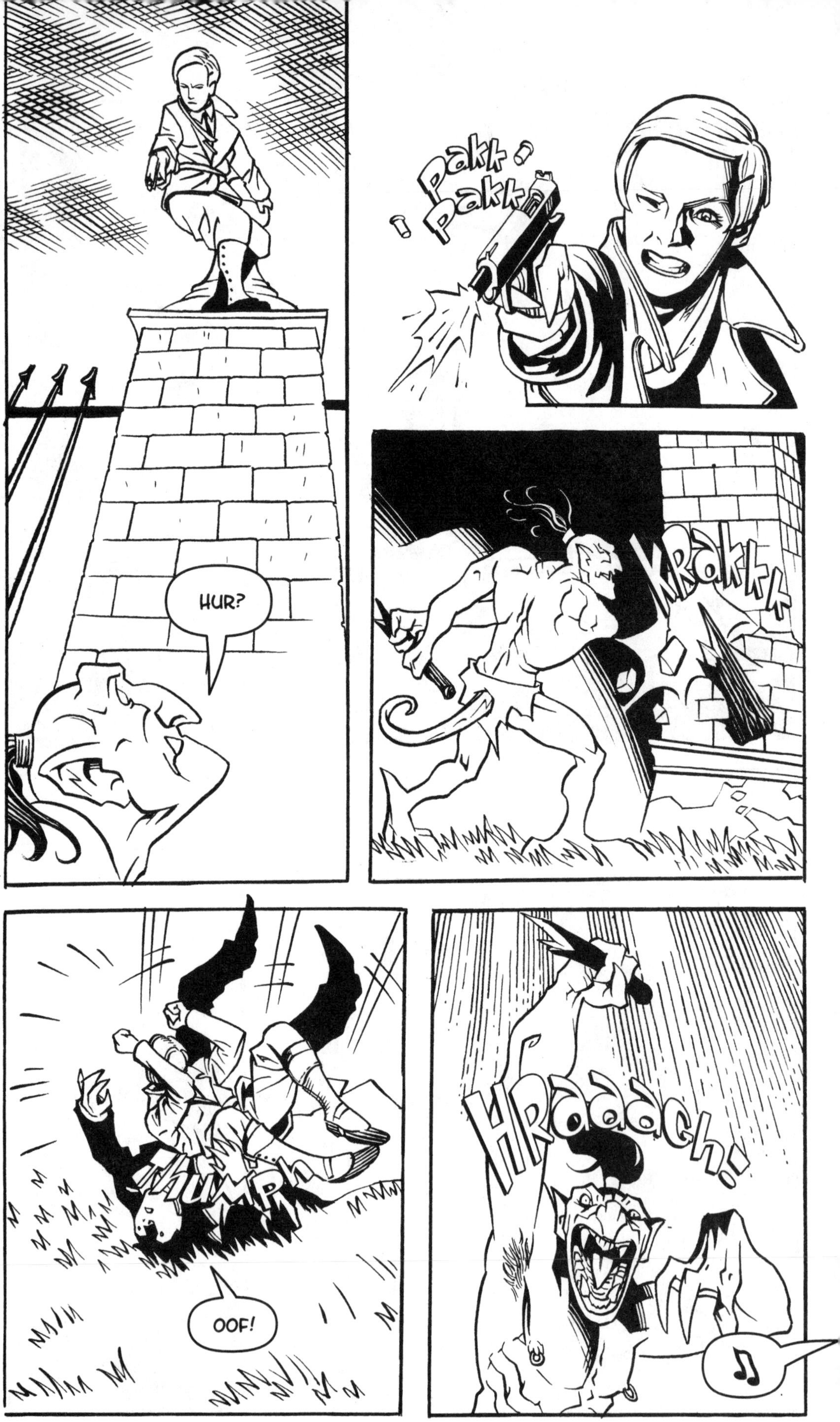
PAKK PAKK
HUR?
KRAKKK
THUMPH
OOF!
HRAAACH!
♪

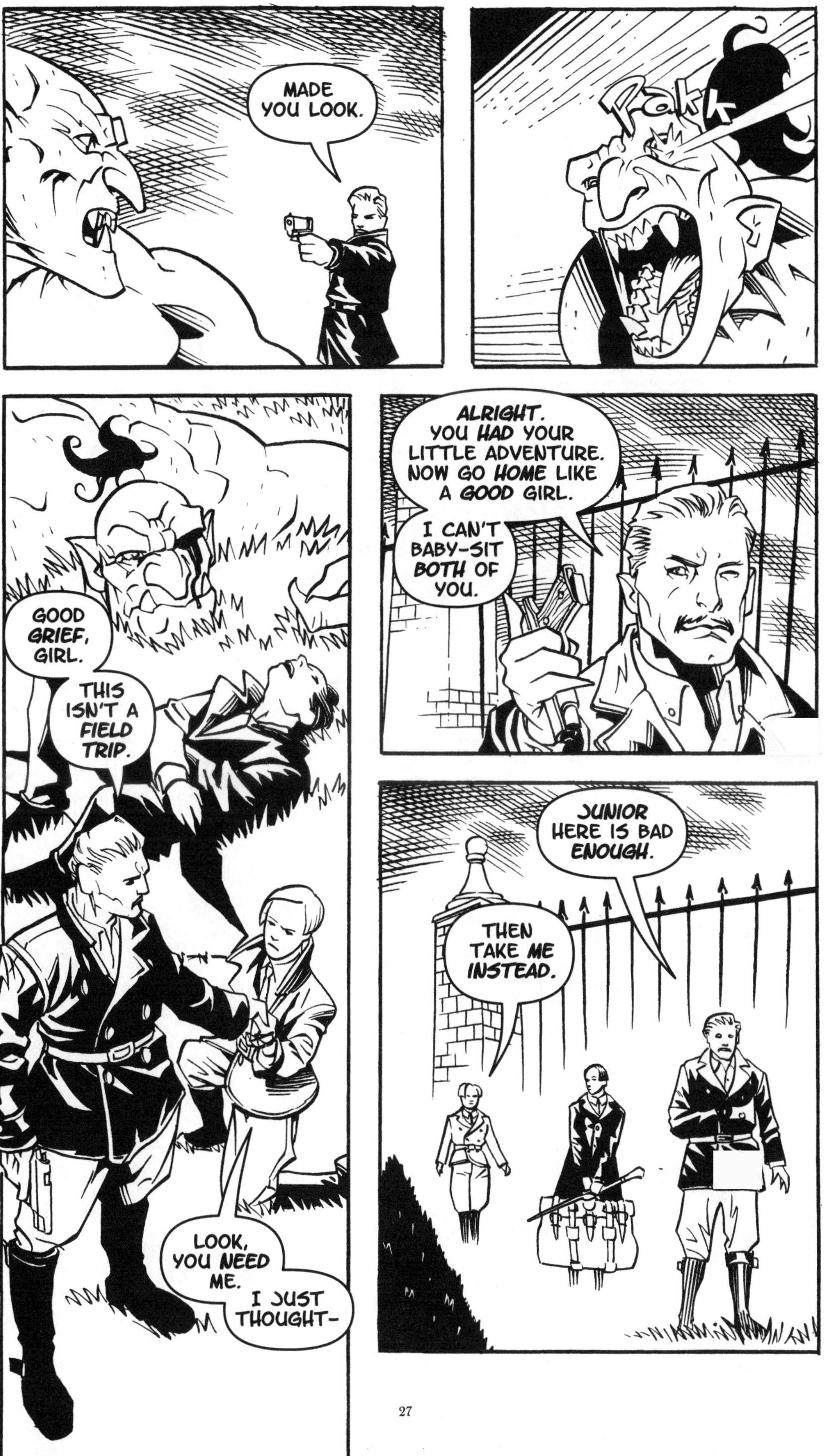

MADE YOU LOOK.
PAKK
GOOD GRIEF, GIRL.
THIS ISN'T A FIELD TRIP.
LOOK, YOU NEED ME.
I JUST THOUGHT-
ALRIGHT. YOU HAD YOUR LITTLE ADVENTURE. NOW GO HOME LIKE A GOOD GIRL.
I CAN'T BABY-SIT BOTH OF YOU.
JUNIOR HERE IS BAD ENOUGH.
THEN TAKE ME INSTEAD.

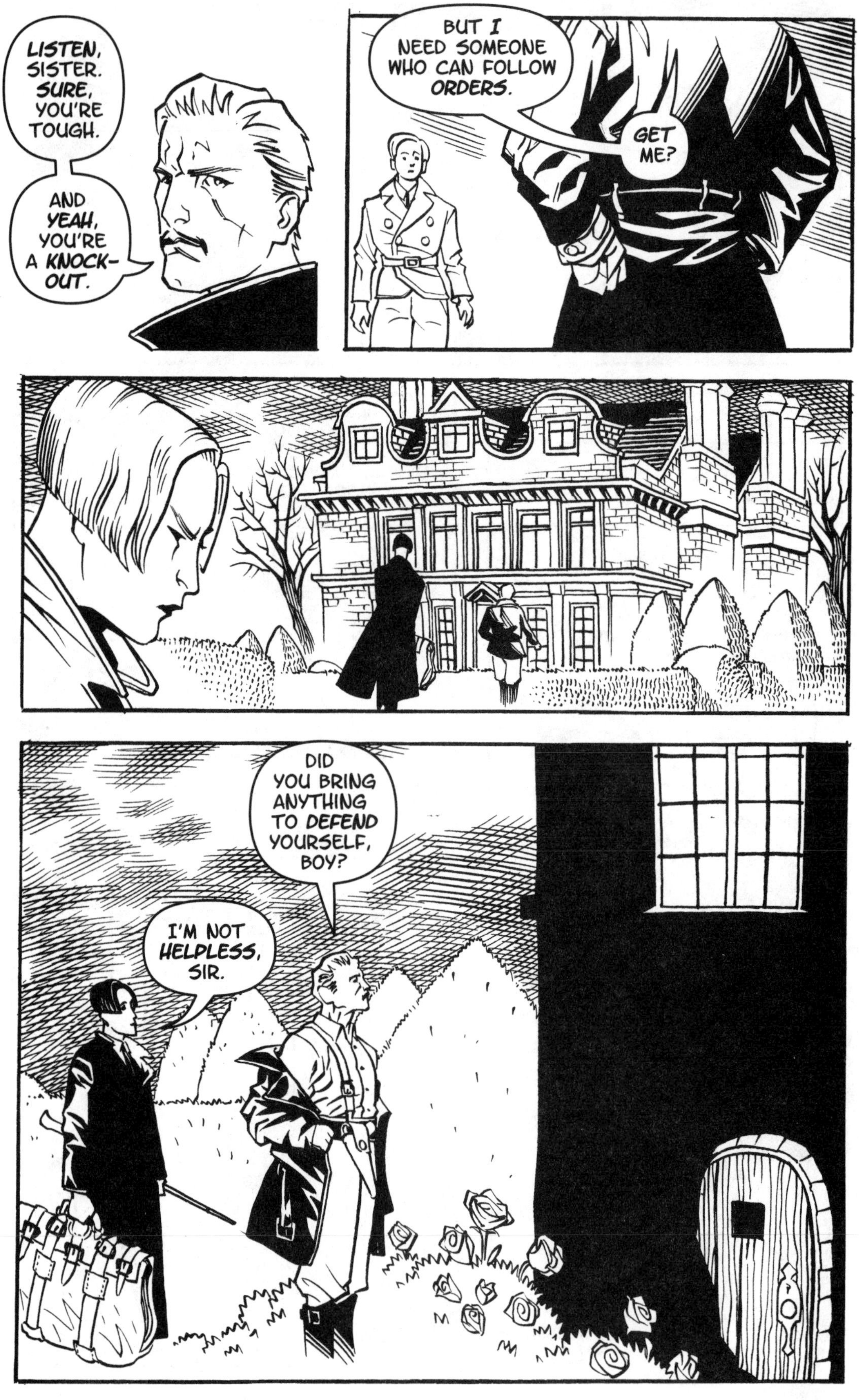
LISTEN, SISTER. SURE, YOU'RE TOUGH.
AND YEAH, YOU'RE A KNOCK-OUT.
BUT I NEED SOMEONE WHO CAN FOLLOW ORDERS.
GET ME?
DID YOU BRING ANYTHING TO DEFEND YOURSELF, BOY?
I'M NOT HELPLESS, SIR.

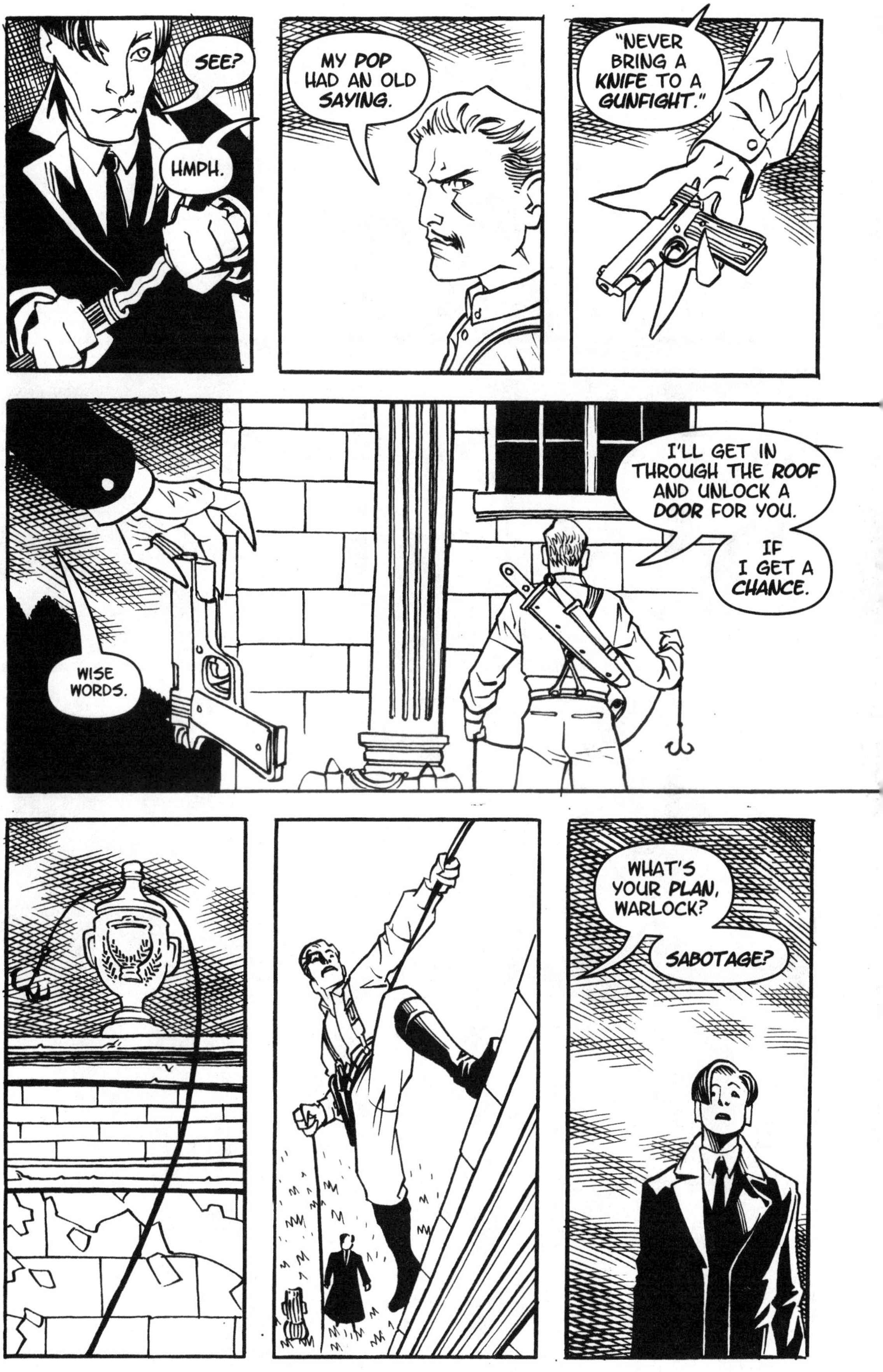
SEE?
HMPH.
MY POP HAD AN OLD SAYING.
"NEVER BRING A KNIFE TO A GUNFIGHT."
I'LL GET IN THROUGH THE ROOF AND UNLOCK A DOOR FOR YOU.
IF I GET A CHANCE.
WISE WORDS.
WHAT'S YOUR PLAN, WARLOCK?
SABOTAGE?

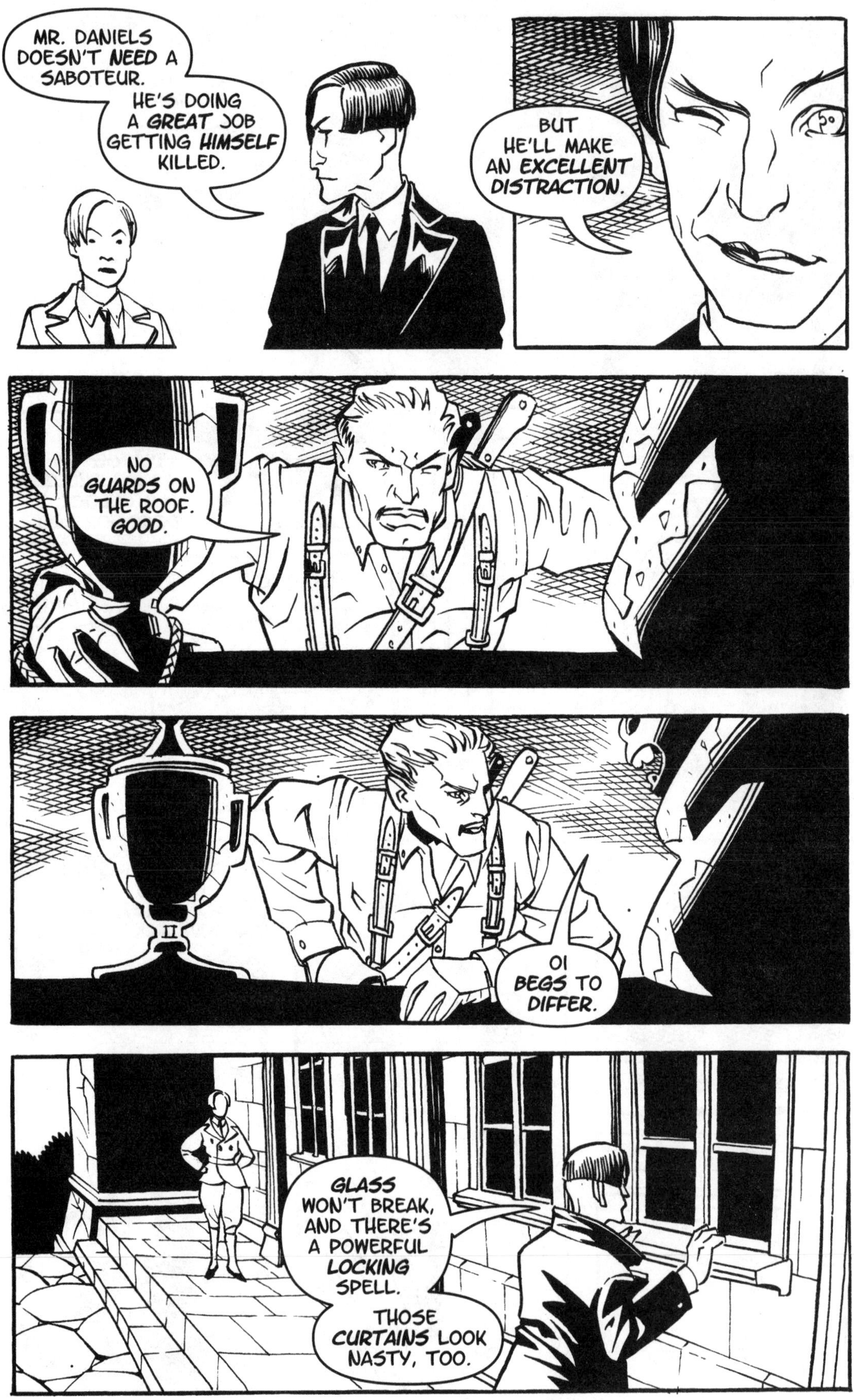
MR. DANIELS DOESN'T NEED A SABOTEUR.
HE'S DOING A GREAT JOB GETTING HIMSELF KILLED.
BUT HE'LL MAKE AN EXCELLENT DISTRACTION.
NO GUARDS ON THE ROOF. GOOD.
OI BEGS TO DIFFER.
GLASS WON'T BREAK, AND THERE'S A POWERFUL LOCKING SPELL.
THOSE CURTAINS LOOK NASTY, TOO.

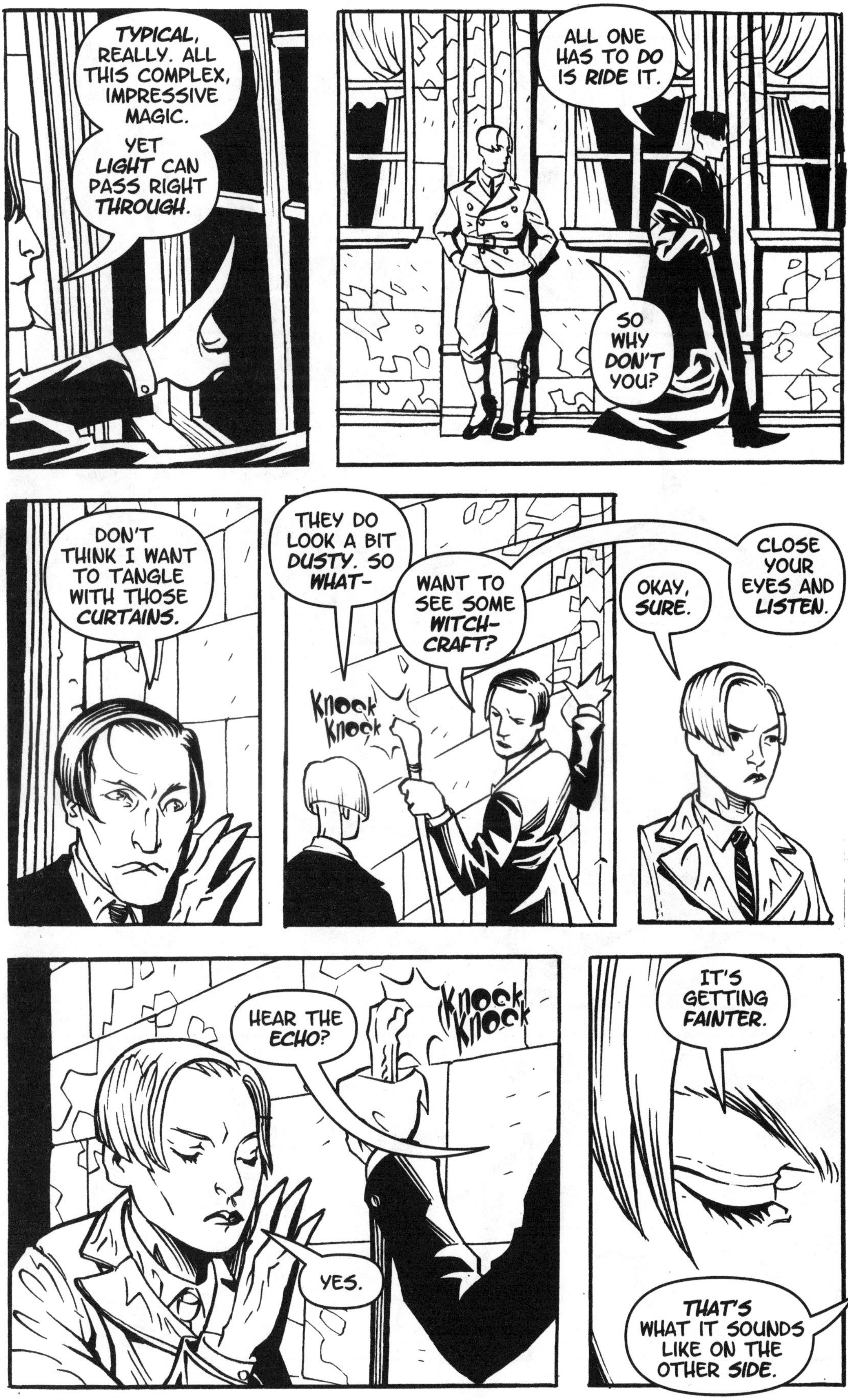
TYPICAL, REALLY. ALL THIS COMPLEX, IMPRESSIVE MAGIC.
YET LIGHT CAN PASS RIGHT THROUGH.
ALL ONE HAS TO DO IS RIDE IT.
SO WHY DON'T YOU?
DON'T THINK I WANT TO TANGLE WITH THOSE CURTAINS.
THEY DO LOOK A BIT DUSTY. SO WHAT-
KNOCK KNOCK
WANT TO SEE SOME WITCH-CRAFT?
CLOSE YOUR EYES AND LISTEN.
OKAY, SURE.
HEAR THE ECHO?
KNOCK KNOCK
YES.
IT'S GETTING FAINTER.
THAT'S WHAT IT SOUNDS LIKE ON THE OTHER SIDE.

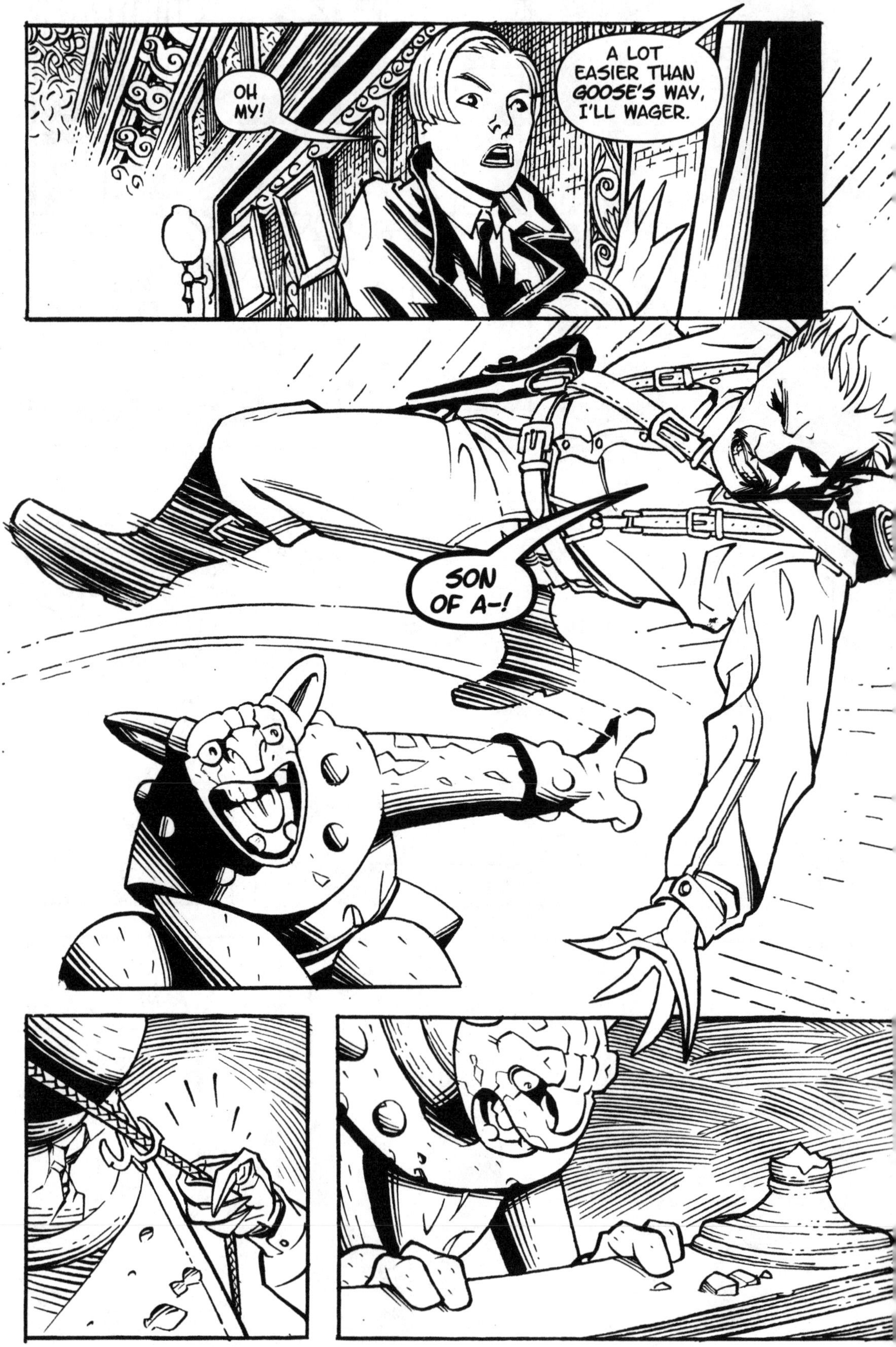
OH MY!
A LOT EASIER THAN GOOSE'S WAY, I'LL WAGER.
SON OF A-!

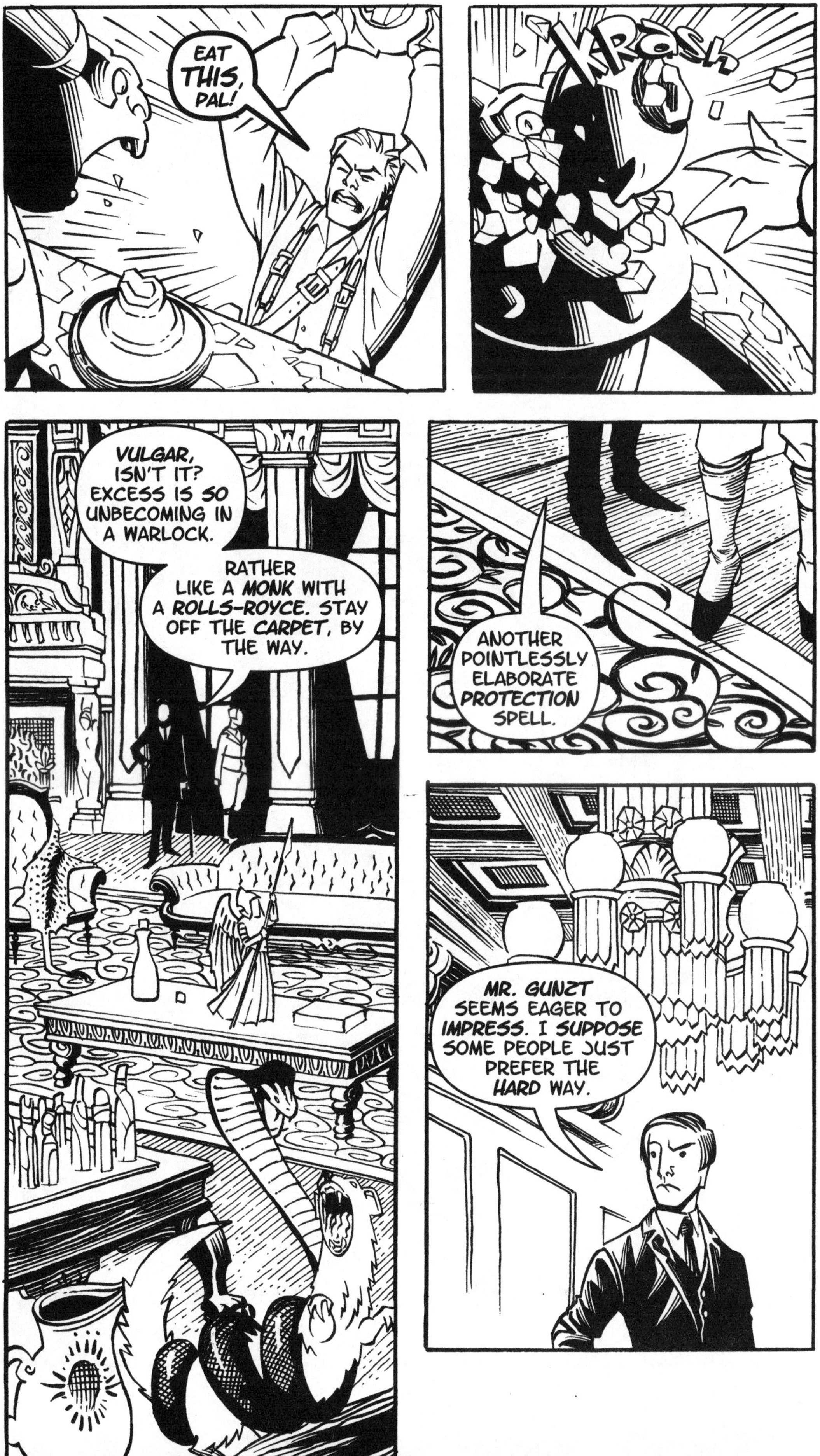
EAT THIS, PAL!
KRASH
VULGAR, ISN'T IT? EXCESS IS SO UNBECOMING IN A WARLOCK.
RATHER LIKE A MONK WITH A ROLLS-ROYCE. STAY OFF THE CARPET, BY THE WAY.
ANOTHER POINTLESSLY ELABORATE PROTECTION SPELL.
MR. GUNZT SEEMS EAGER TO IMPRESS. I SUPPOSE SOME PEOPLE JUST PREFER THE HARD WAY.

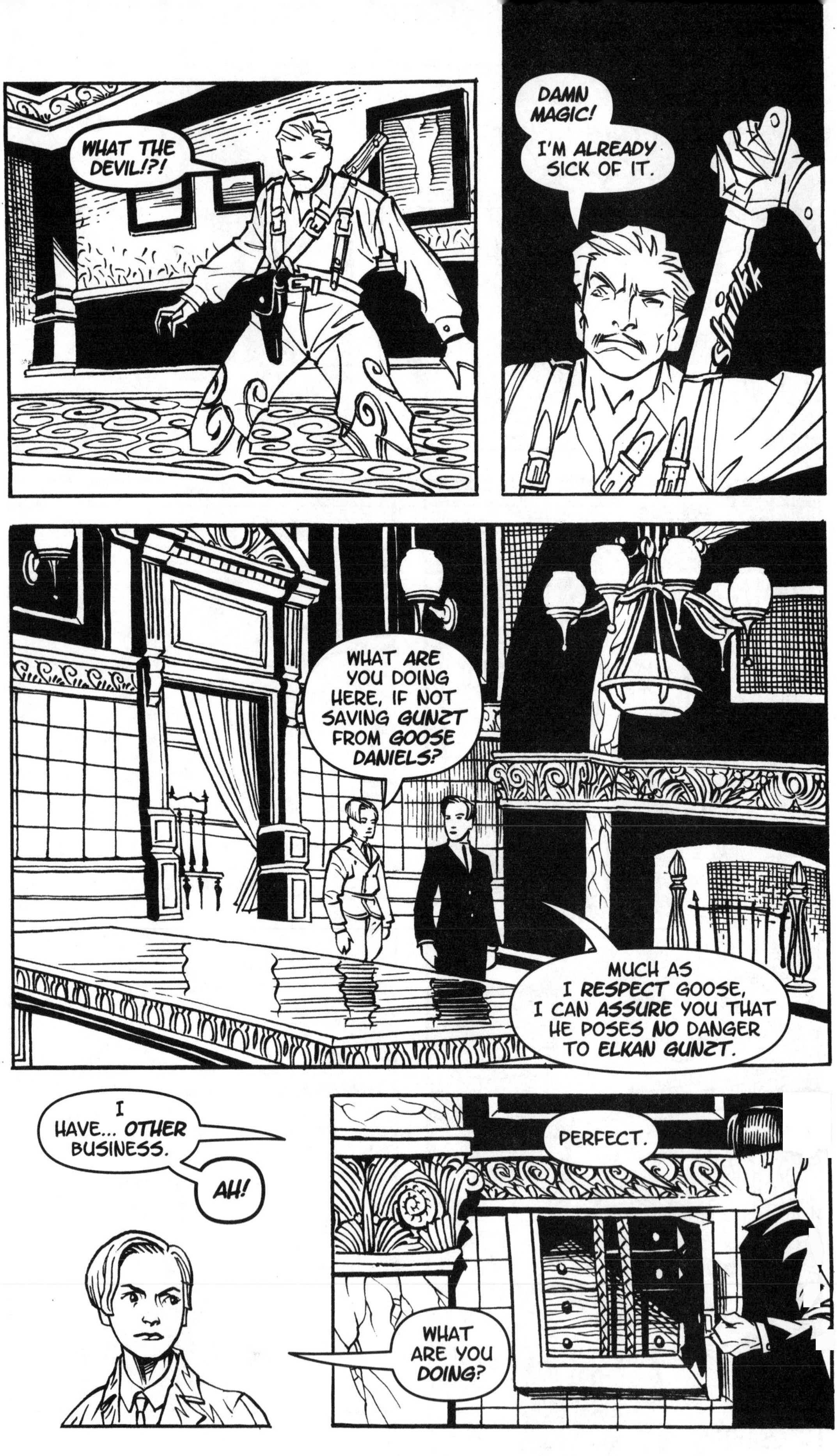

WHAT THE DEVIL!?!
DAMN MAGIC!
I'M ALREADY SICK OF IT.
shinkk
WHAT ARE YOU DOING HERE, IF NOT SAVING GUNZT FROM GOOSE DANIELS?
MUCH AS I RESPECT GOOSE, I CAN ASSURE YOU THAT HE POSES NO DANGER TO ELKAN GUNZT.
I HAVE... OTHER BUSINESS.
AH!
PERFECT.
WHAT ARE YOU DOING?

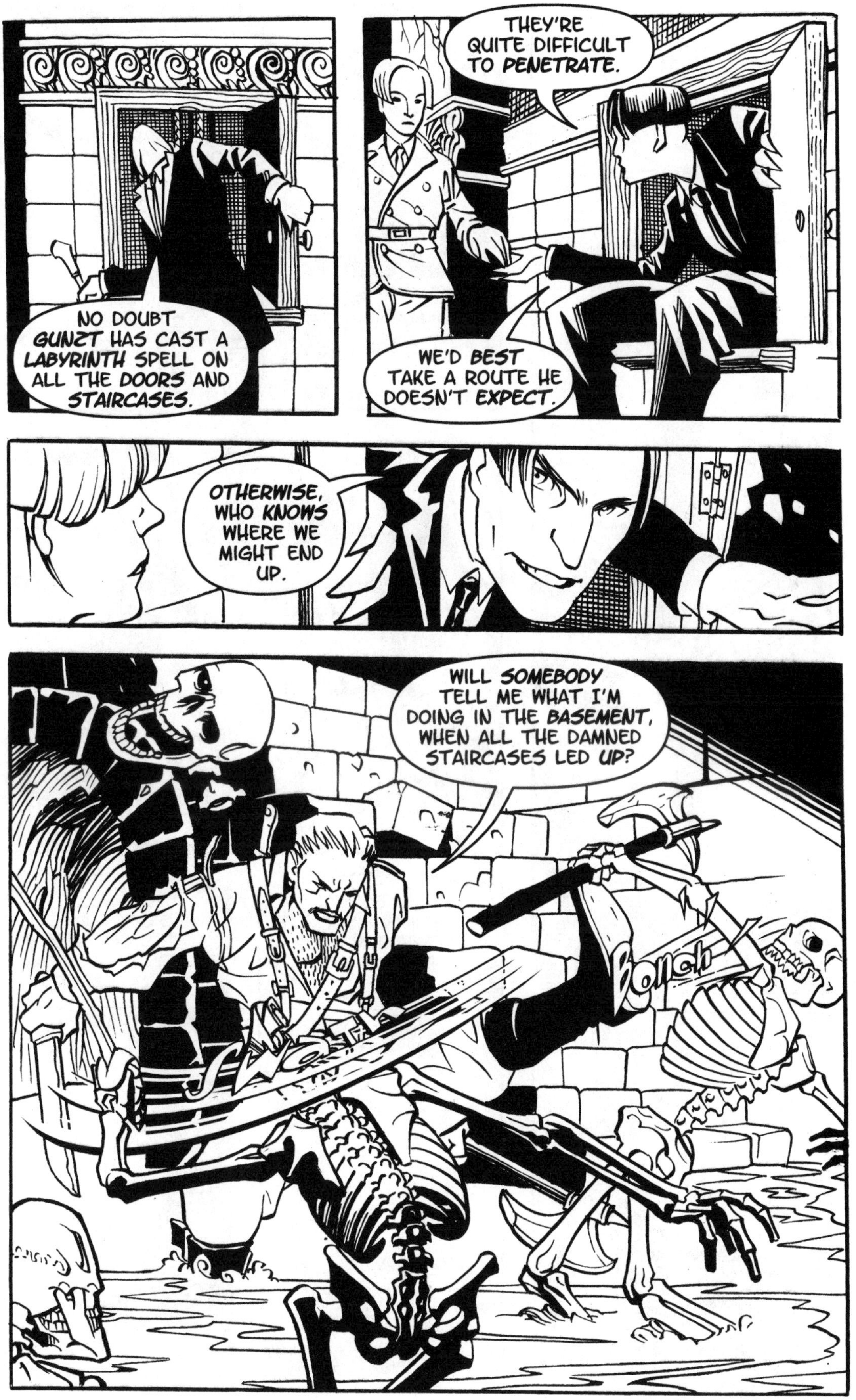
NO DOUBT GUNZT HAS CAST A LABYRINTH SPELL ON ALL THE DOORS AND STAIRCASES.
THEY'RE QUITE DIFFICULT TO PENETRATE.
WE'D BEST TAKE A ROUTE HE DOESN'T EXPECT.
OTHERWISE, WHO KNOWS WHERE WE MIGHT END UP.
WILL SOMEBODY TELL ME WHAT I'M DOING IN THE BASEMENT, WHEN ALL THE DAMNED STAIRCASES LED UP?

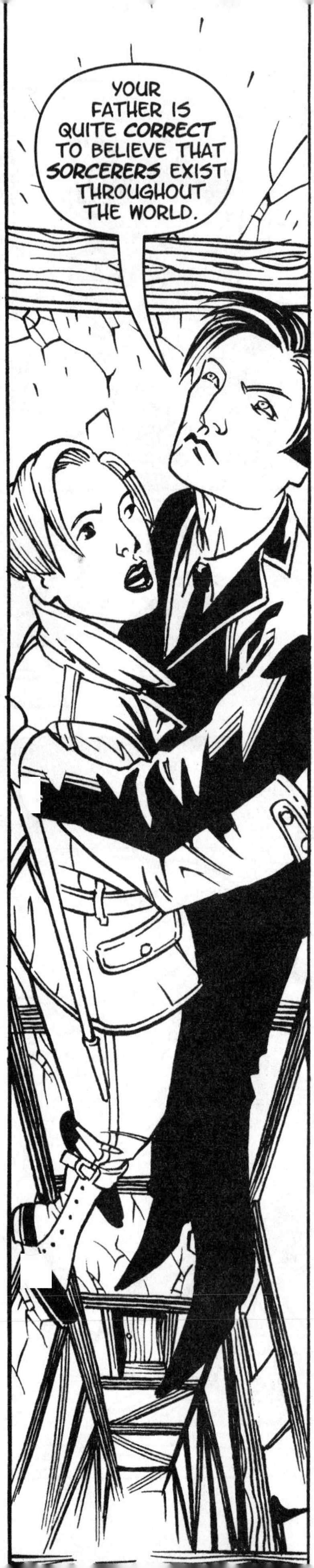
YOUR FATHER IS QUITE CORRECT TO BELIEVE THAT SORCERERS EXIST THROUGHOUT THE WORLD.

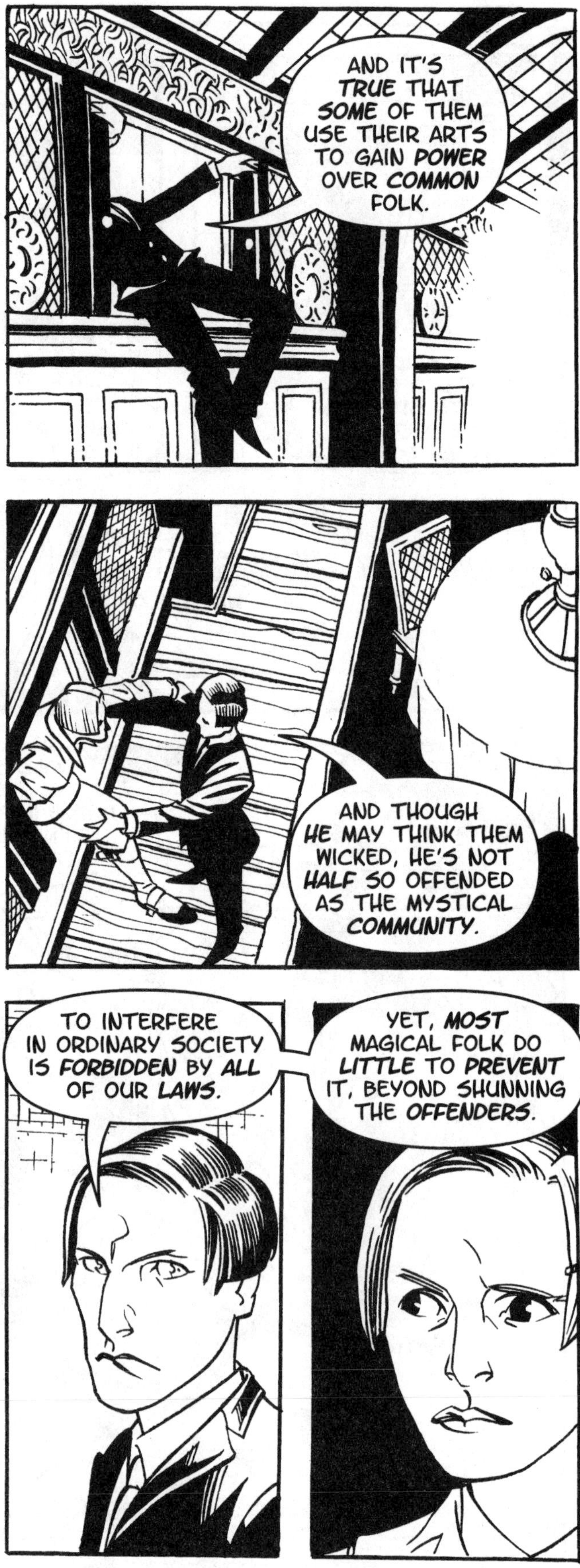
AND IT'S TRUE THAT SOME OF THEM USE THEIR ARTS TO GAIN POWER OVER COMMON FOLK.
AND THOUGH HE MAY THINK THEM WICKED, HE'S NOT HALF SO OFFENDED AS THE MYSTICAL COMMUNITY.
TO INTERFERE IN ORDINARY SOCIETY IS FORBIDDEN BY ALL OF OUR LAWS.
YET, MOST MAGICAL FOLK DO LITTLE TO PREVENT IT, BEYOND SHUNNING THE OFFENDERS.

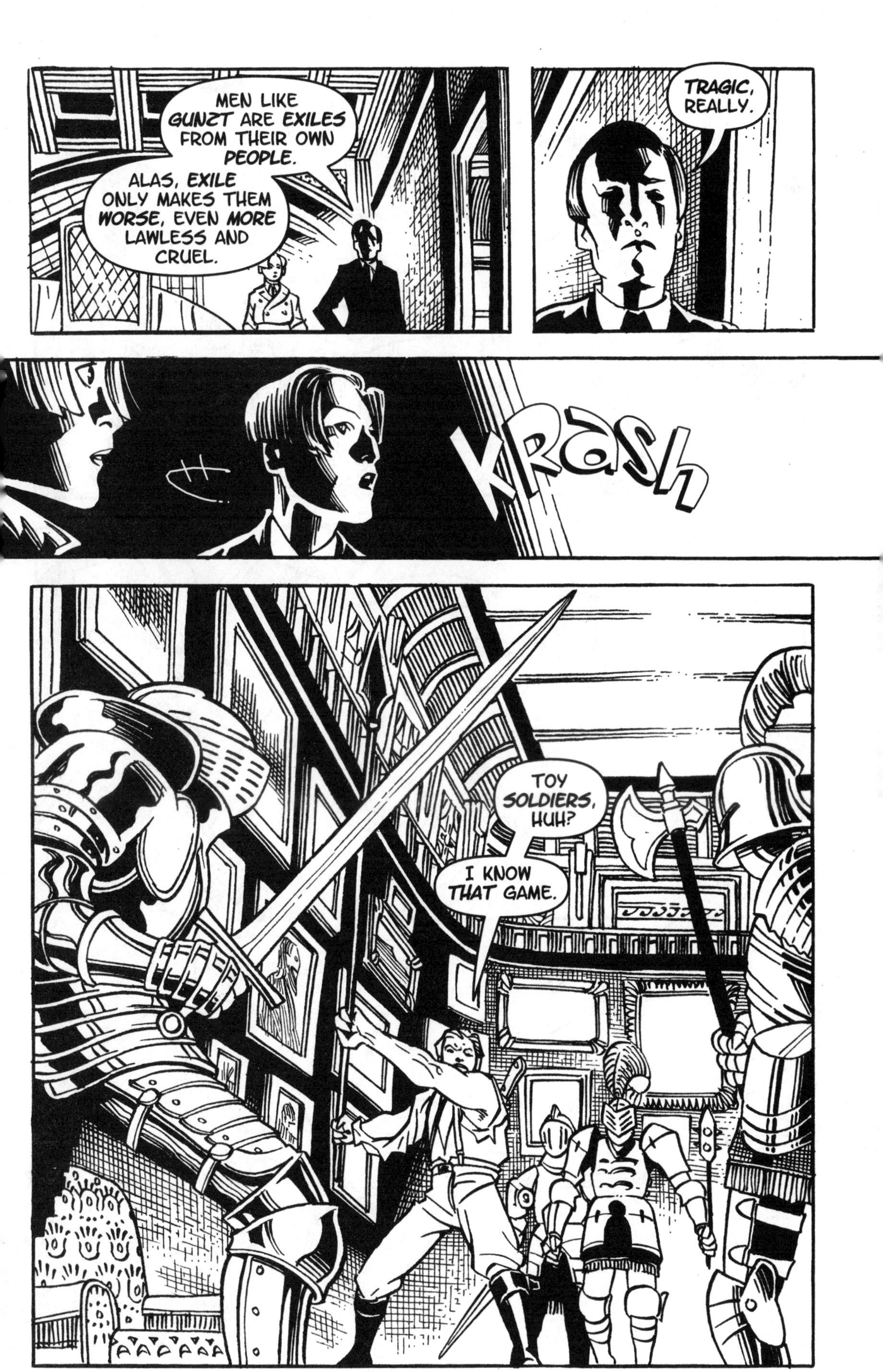
MEN LIKE GUNZT ARE EXILES FROM THEIR OWN PEOPLE.
ALAS, EXILE ONLY MAKES THEM WORSE, EVEN MORE LAWLESS AND CRUEL.
TRAGIC, REALLY.
KRASH
TOY SOLDIERS, HUH?
I KNOW THAT GAME.

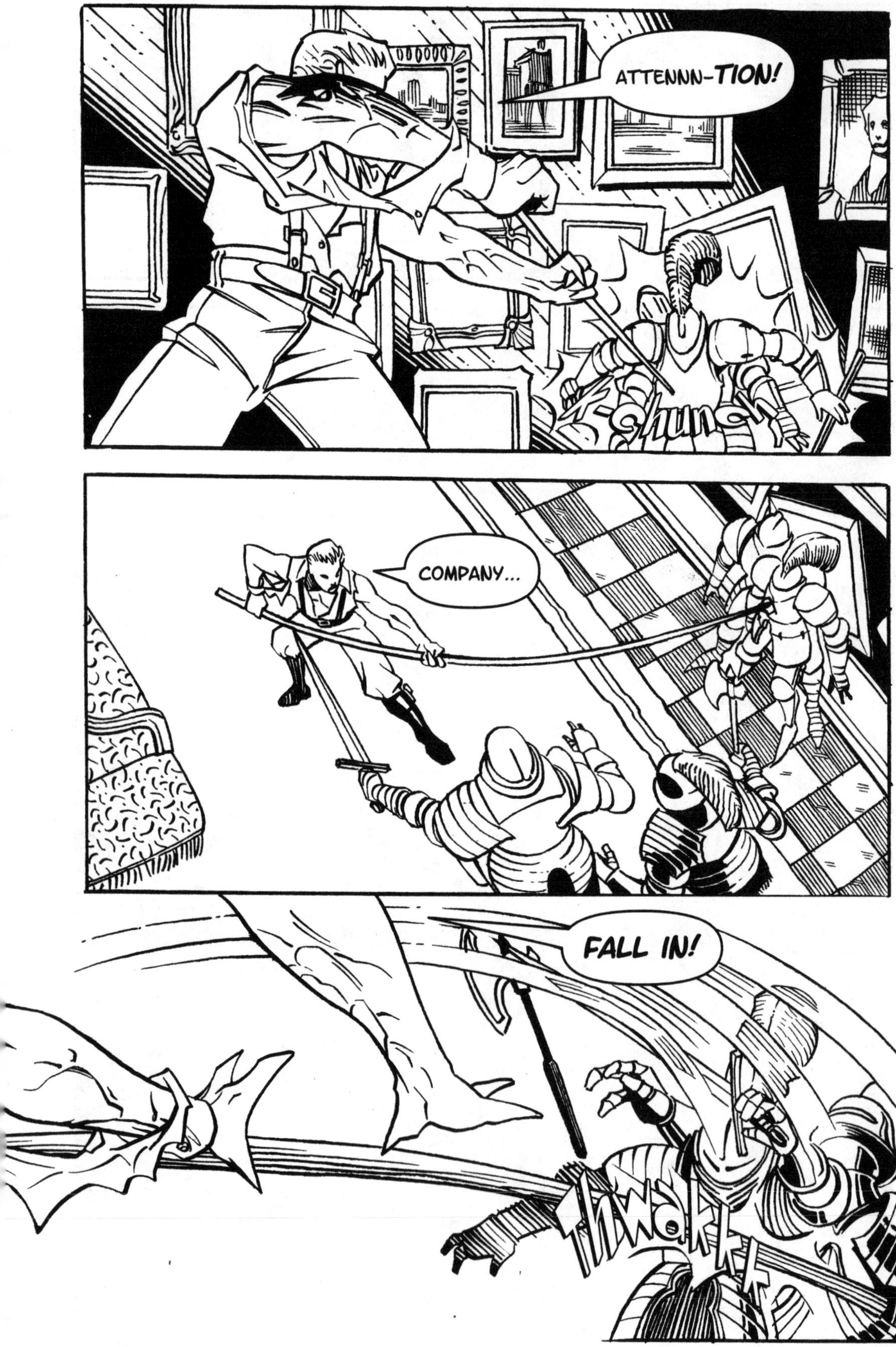
ATTENNN-TION!
K-CHUNCH
COMPANY...
FALL IN!
THWAKK

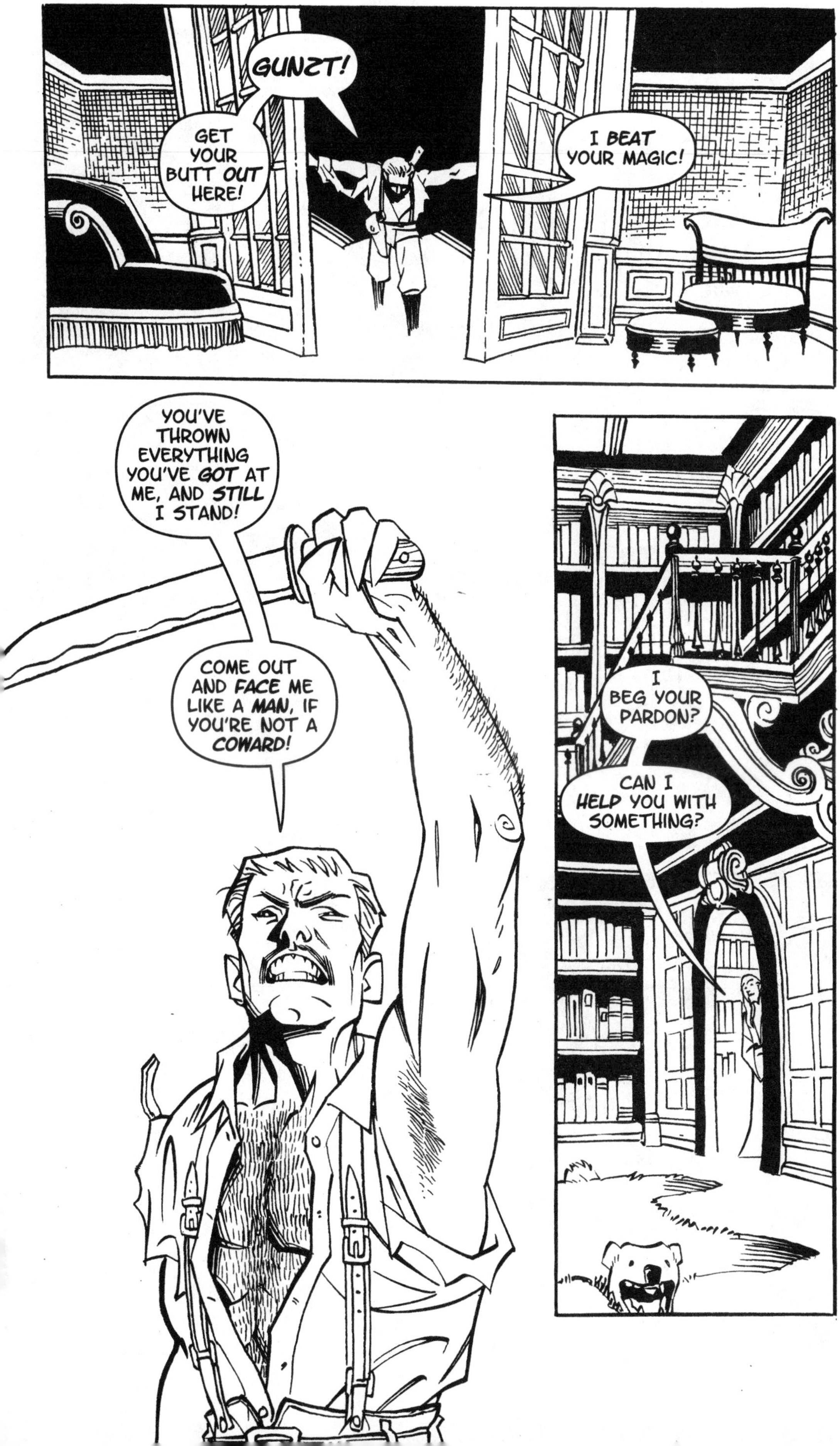
GUNZT!
GET YOUR BUTT OUT HERE!
I BEAT YOUR MAGIC!
YOU'VE THROWN EVERYTHING YOU'VE GOT AT ME, AND STILL I STAND!
COME OUT AND FACE ME LIKE A MAN, IF YOU'RE NOT A COWARD!
I BEG YOUR PARDON?
CAN I HELP YOU WITH SOMETHING?

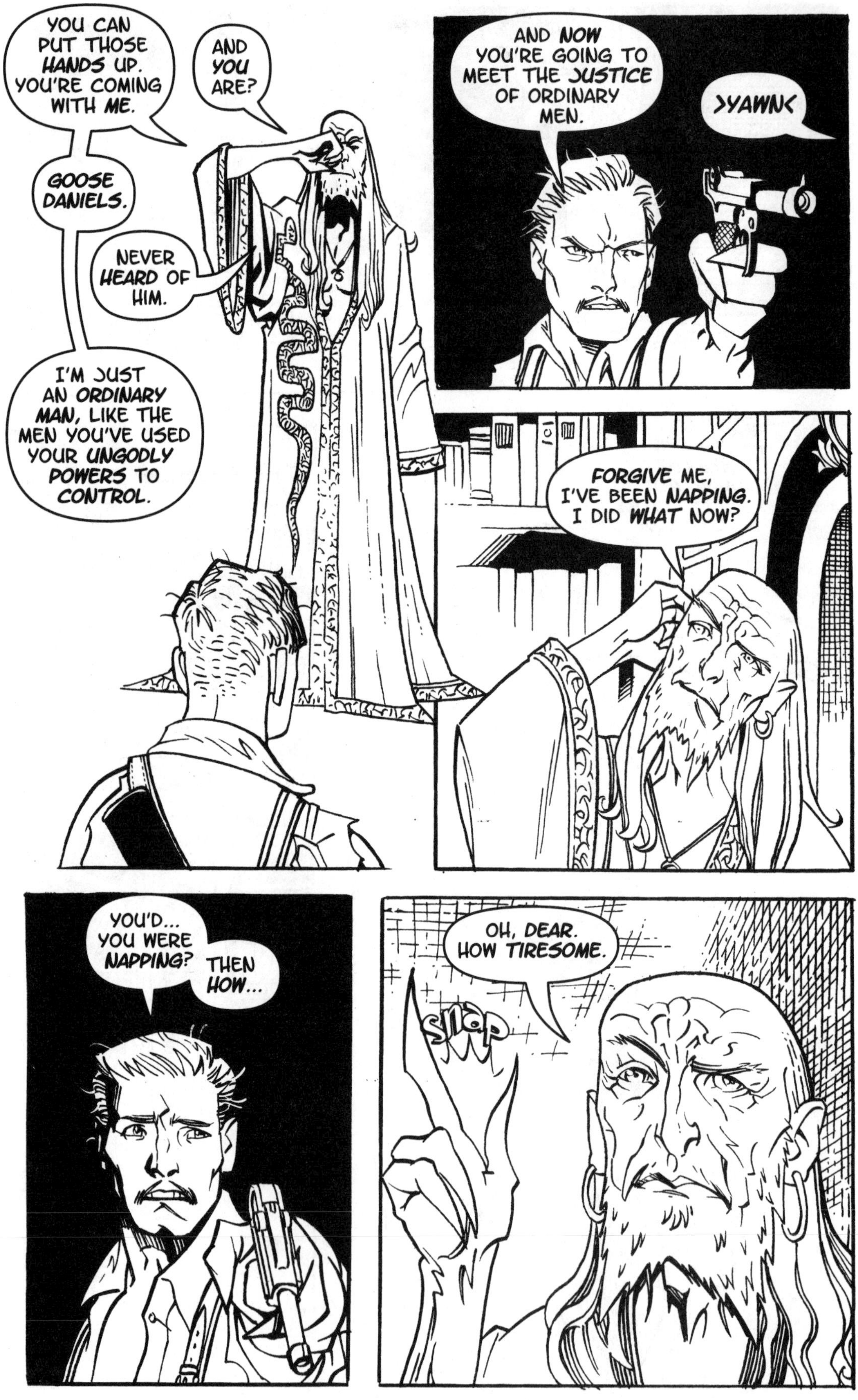
YOU CAN PUT THOSE HANDS UP. YOU'RE COMING WITH ME.
AND YOU ARE?
GOOSE DANIELS.
NEVER HEARD OF HIM.
I'M JUST AN ORDINARY MAN, LIKE THE MEN YOU'VE USED YOUR UNGODLY POWERS TO CONTROL.
AND NOW YOU'RE GOING TO MEET THE JUSTICE OF ORDINARY MEN.
>YAWN<
FORGIVE ME, I'VE BEEN NAPPING. I DID WHAT NOW?
YOU'D... YOU WERE NAPPING?
THEN HOW...
OH, DEAR. HOW TIRESOME.
SNAP

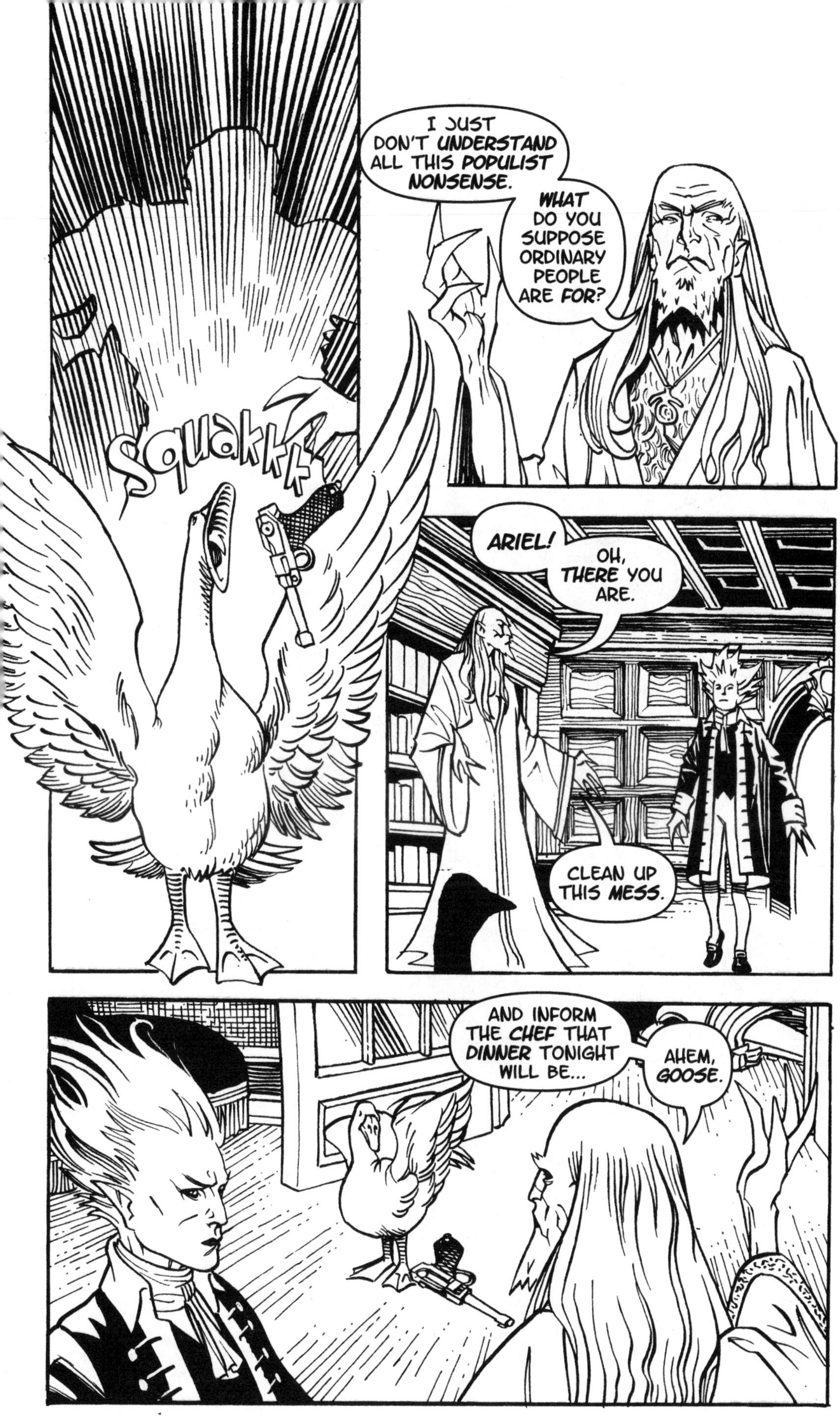
SQUAKKK
I JUST DON'T UNDERSTAND ALL THIS POPULIST NONSENSE.
WHAT DO YOU SUPPOSE ORDINARY PEOPLE ARE FOR?
ARIEL!
OH, THERE YOU ARE.
CLEAN UP THIS MESS.
AND INFORM THE CHEF THAT DINNER TONIGHT WILL BE...
AHEM, GOOSE.

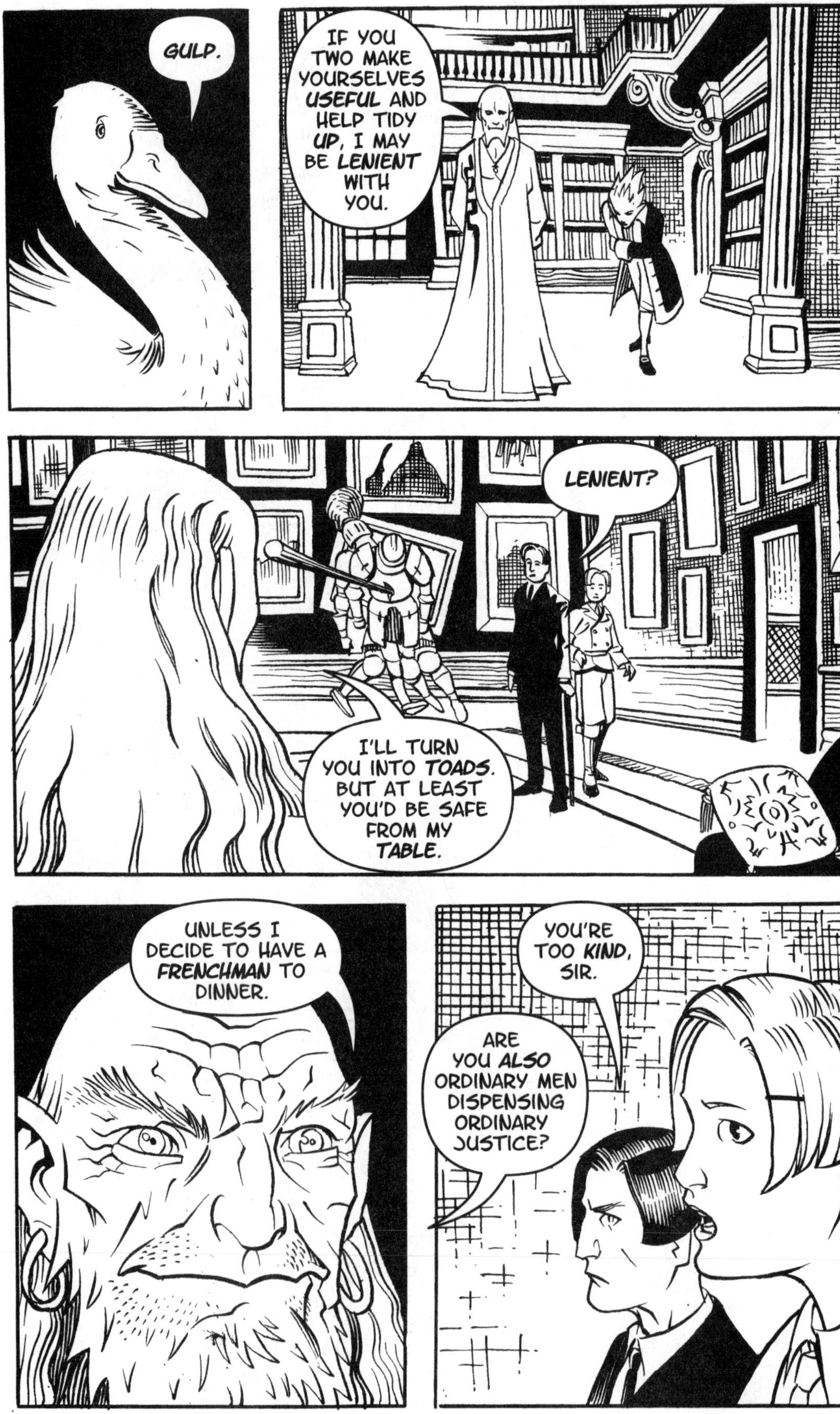
GULP.
IF YOU TWO MAKE YOURSELVES USEFUL AND HELP TIDY UP, I MAY BE LENIENT WITH YOU.
LENIENT?
I'LL TURN YOU INTO TOADS. BUT AT LEAST YOU'D BE SAFE FROM MY TABLE.
UNLESS I DECIDE TO HAVE A FRENCHMAN TO DINNER.
YOU'RE TOO KIND, SIR.
ARE YOU ALSO ORDINARY MEN DISPENSING ORDINARY JUSTICE?

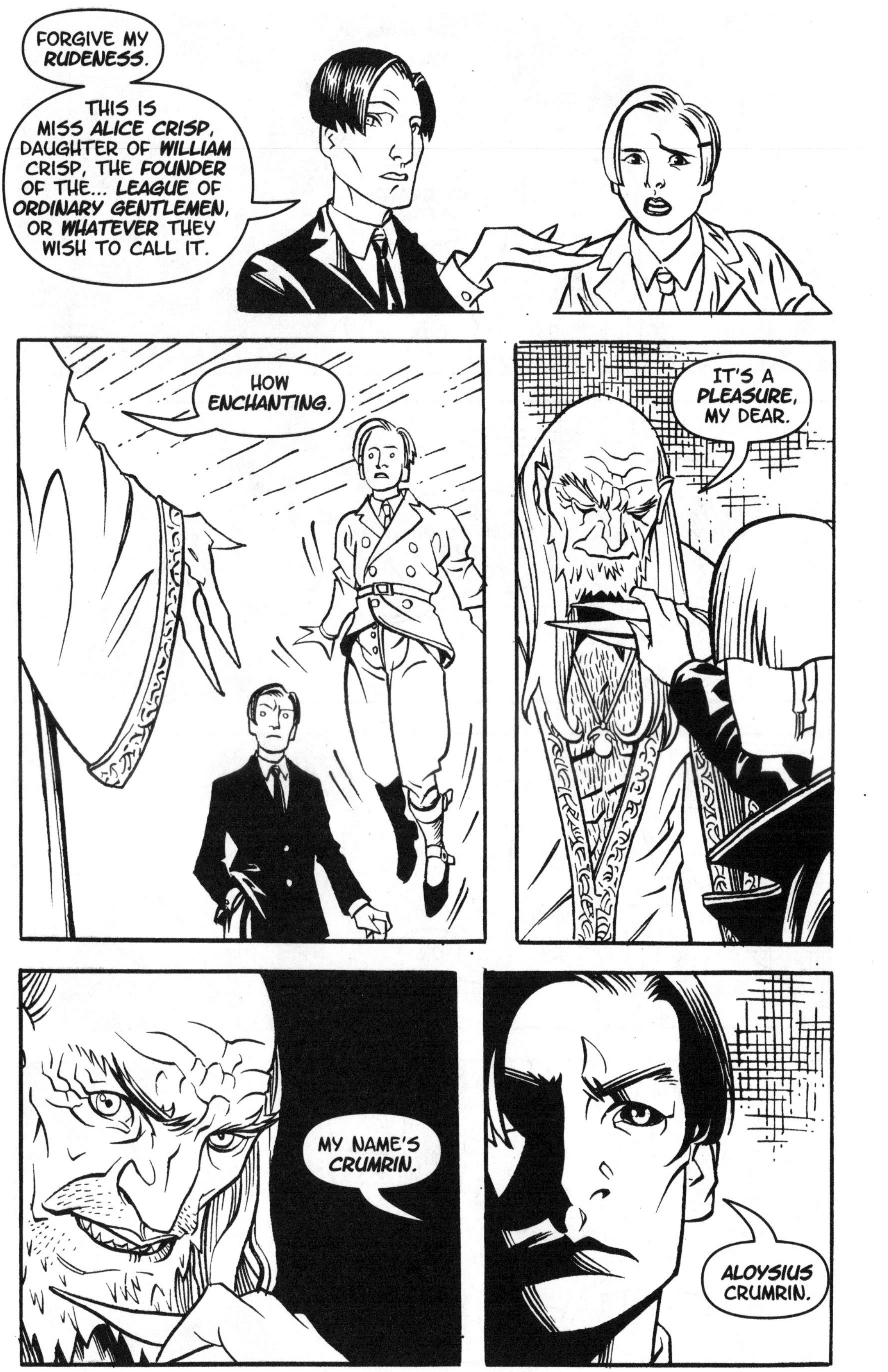
FORGIVE MY RUDENESS.
THIS IS MISS ALICE CRISP, DAUGHTER OF WILLIAM CRISP, THE FOUNDER OF THE... LEAGUE OF ORDINARY GENTLEMEN, OR WHATEVER THEY WISH TO CALL IT.
HOW ENCHANTING.
IT'S A PLEASURE, MY DEAR.
MY NAME'S CRUMRIN.
ALOYSIUS CRUMRIN.

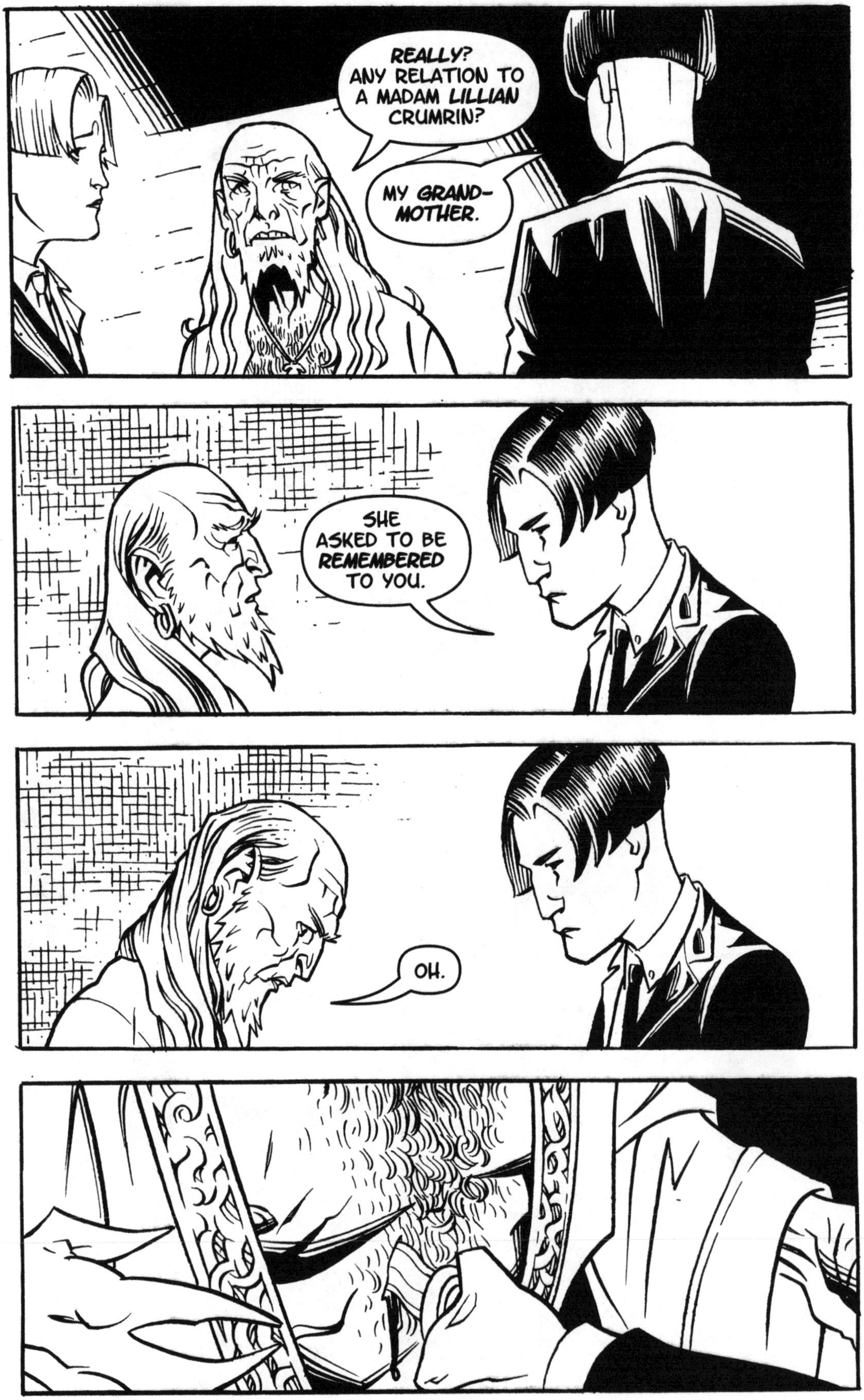
REALLY? ANY RELATION TO A MADAM LILLIAN CRUMRIN?
MY GRAND-MOTHER.
SHE ASKED TO BE REMEMBERED TO YOU.
OH.

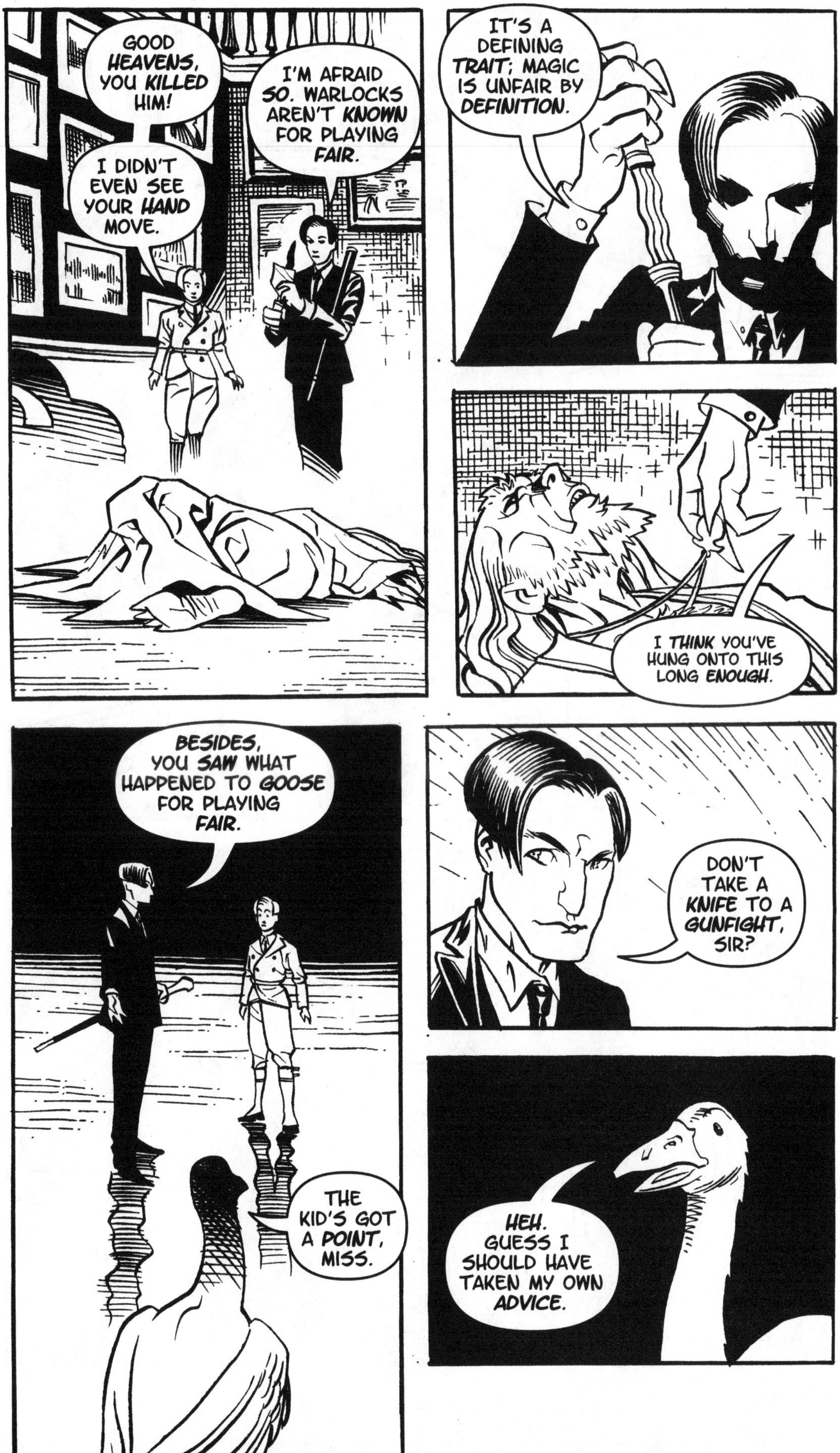
GOOD HEAVENS, YOU KILLED HIM!
I DIDN'T EVEN SEE YOUR HAND MOVE.
I'M AFRAID SO. WARLOCKS AREN'T KNOWN FOR PLAYING FAIR.
IT'S A DEFINING TRAIT; MAGIC IS UNFAIR BY DEFINITION.
I THINK YOU'VE HUNG ONTO THIS LONG ENOUGH.
BESIDES, YOU SAW WHAT HAPPENED TO GOOSE FOR PLAYING FAIR.
THE KID'S GOT A POINT, MISS.
DON'T TAKE A KNIFE TO A GUNFIGHT, SIR?
HEH. GUESS I SHOULD HAVE TAKEN MY OWN ADVICE.

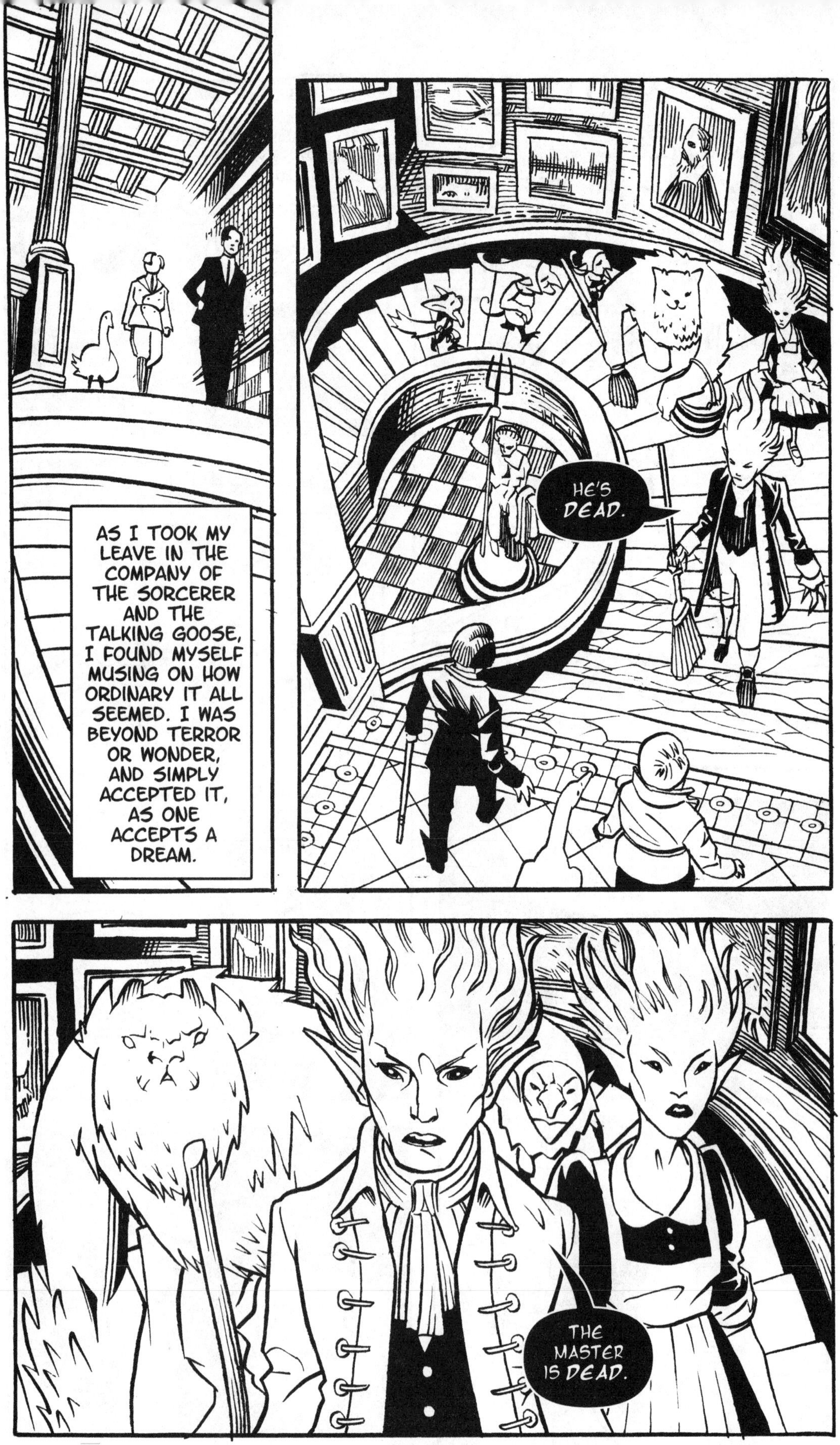
AS I TOOK MY LEAVE IN THE COMPANY OF THE SORCERER AND THE TALKING GOOSE, I FOUND MYSELF MUSING ON HOW ORDINARY IT ALL SEEMED. I WAS BEYOND TERROR OR WONDER, AND SIMPLY ACCEPTED IT, AS ONE ACCEPTS A DREAM.
HE'S DEAD.
THE MASTER IS DEAD.

YOU'RE FREE TO *GO*.

IT WASN'T HUMAN. IT WAS SOMETHING ELSE.

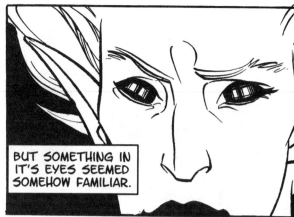

BUT SOMETHING IN IT'S EYES SEEMED SOMEHOW FAMILIAR.

A LOOK OF WOUNDED DIGNITY I'D SEEN IN THE EYE OF MANY AN ORDINARY MAN.

GOODBYE, MISS CRISP.

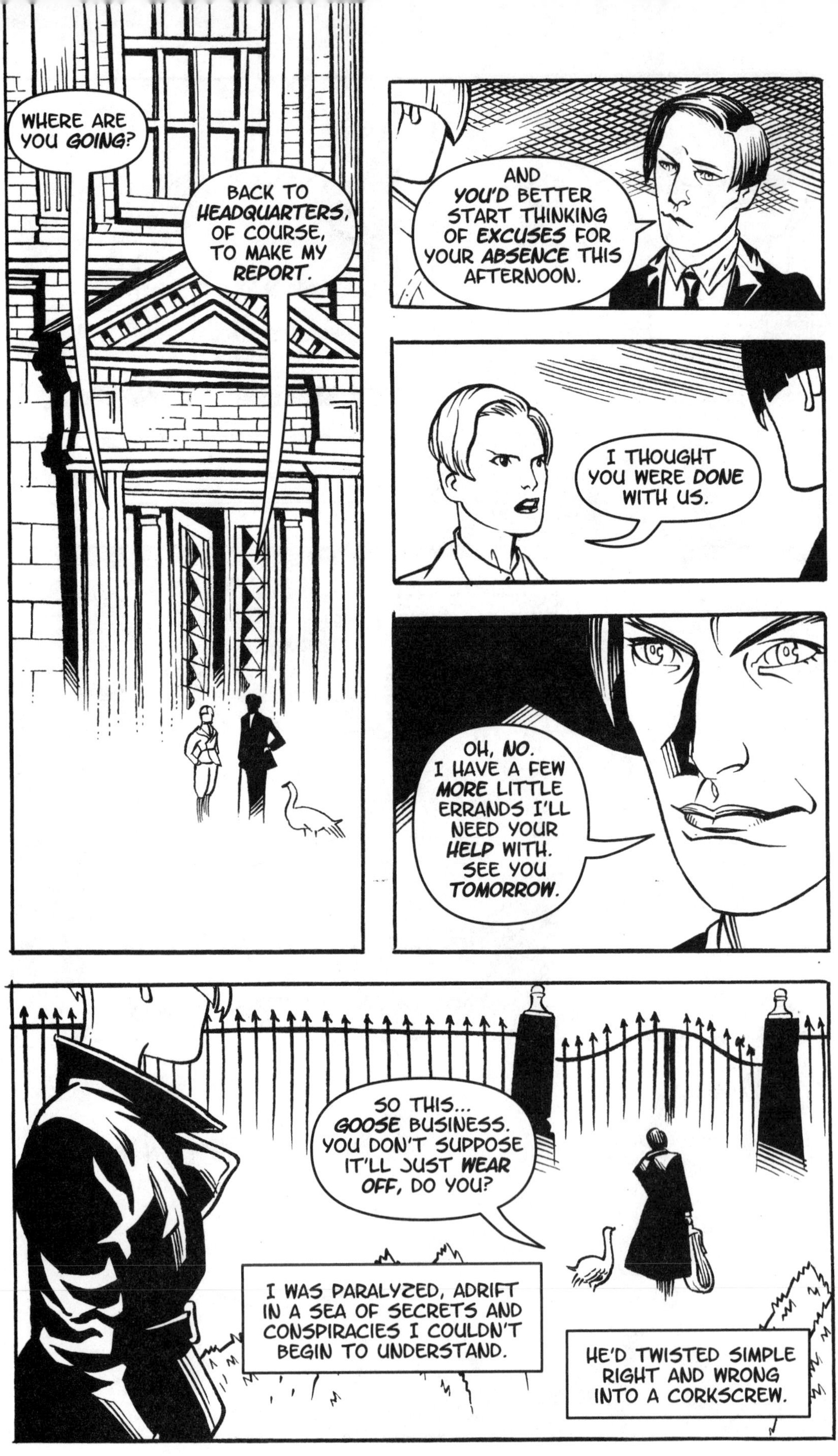
WHERE ARE YOU GOING?
BACK TO HEADQUARTERS, OF COURSE, TO MAKE MY REPORT.
AND YOU'D BETTER START THINKING OF EXCUSES FOR YOUR ABSENCE THIS AFTERNOON.
I THOUGHT YOU WERE DONE WITH US.
OH, NO. I HAVE A FEW MORE LITTLE ERRANDS I'LL NEED YOUR HELP WITH. SEE YOU TOMORROW.
SO THIS... GOOSE BUSINESS. YOU DON'T SUPPOSE IT'LL JUST WEAR OFF, DO YOU?
I WAS PARALYZED, ADRIFT IN A SEA OF SECRETS AND CONSPIRACIES I COULDN'T BEGIN TO UNDERSTAND.
HE'D TWISTED SIMPLE RIGHT AND WRONG INTO A CORKSCREW.

I SUPPOSE THAT'S WHAT SORCERERS DO.

THERE WAS ONLY ONE WAY TO CLEAN UP THE MESS HE'D MADE OF MY MIND.

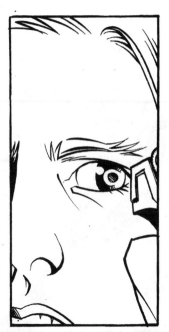

DAMN IT.

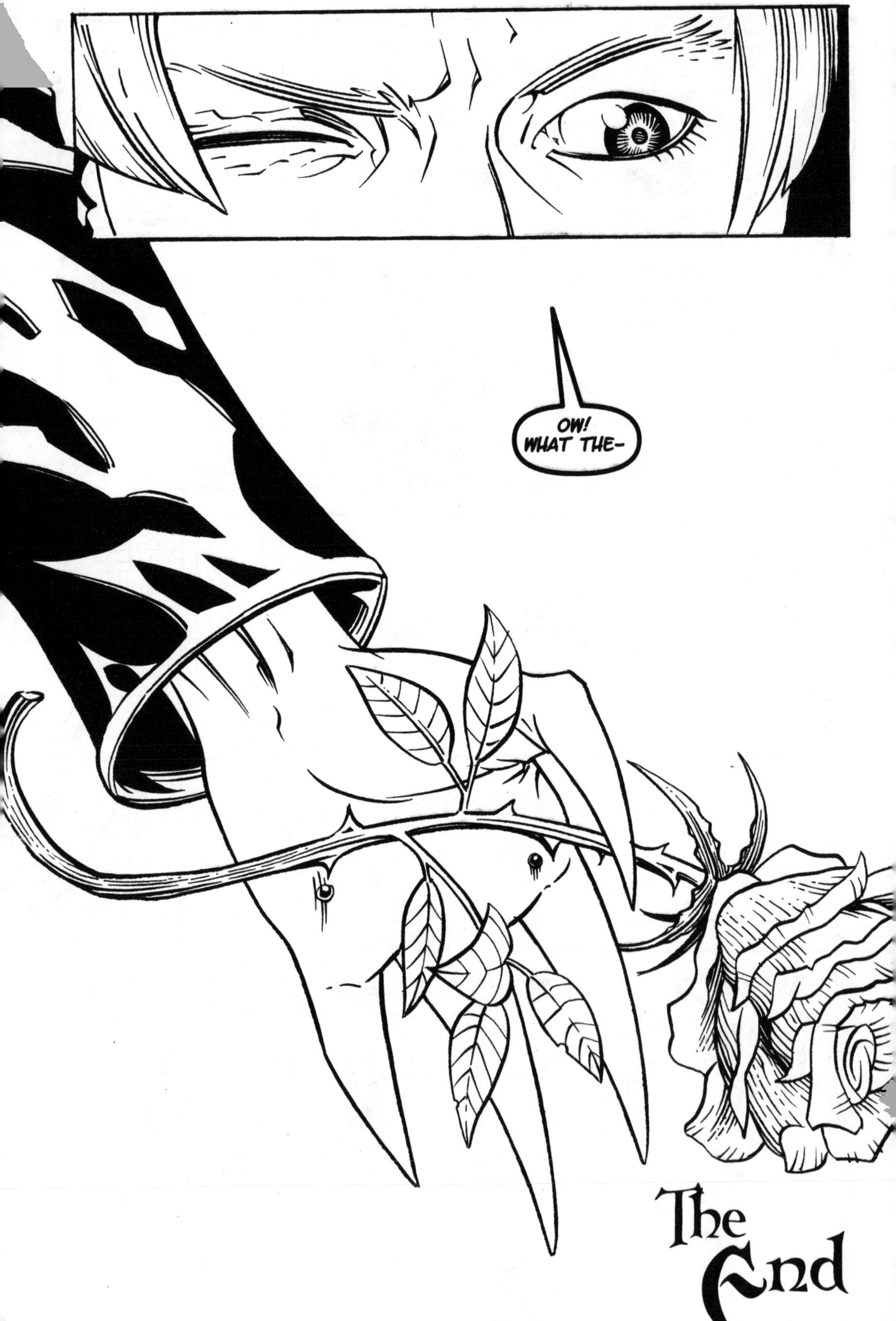
OW!
WHAT THE-
The End

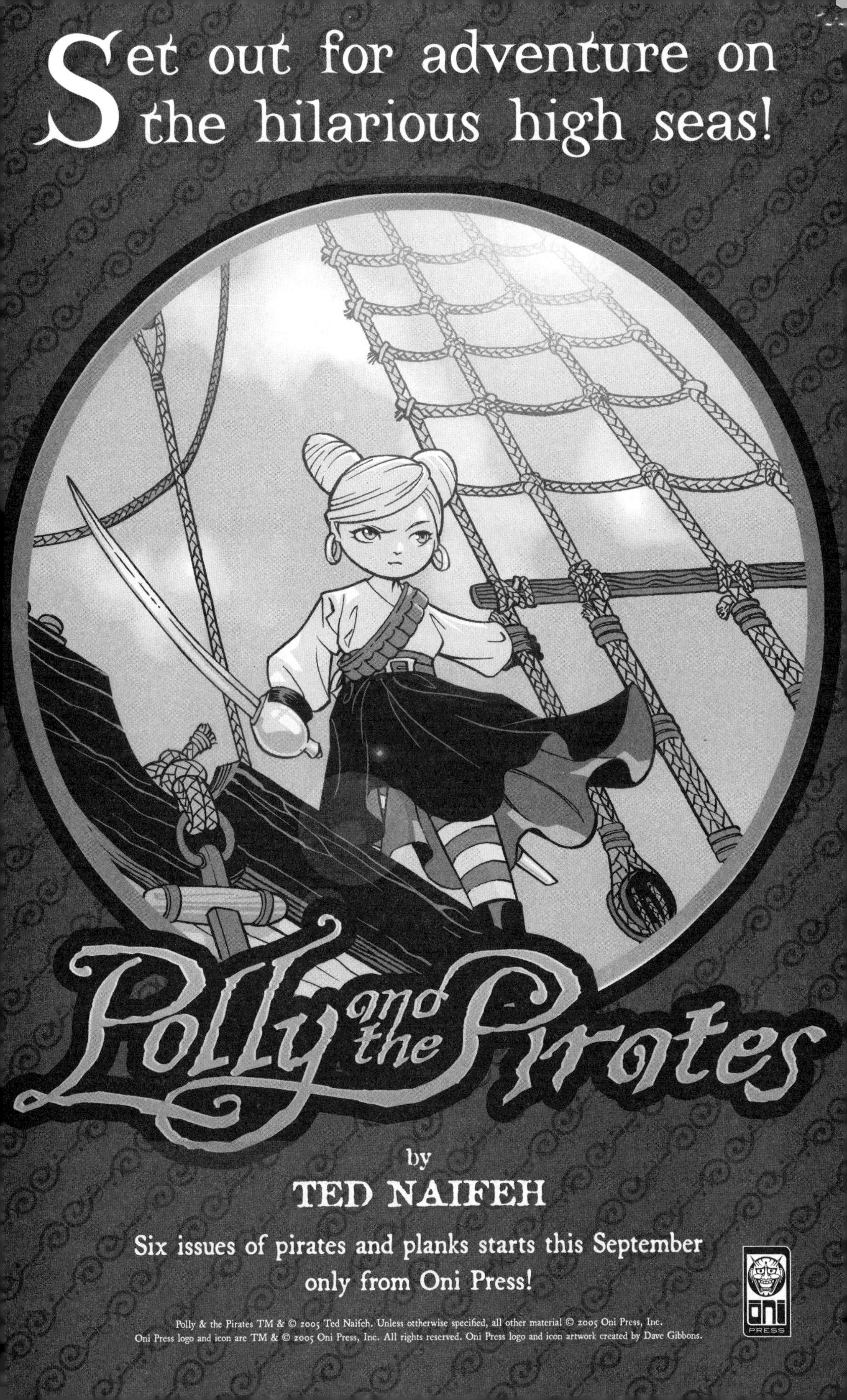
Set out for adventure on the hilarious high seas!
Polly and the Pirates
by
TED NAIFEH
Six issues of pirates and planks starts this September
only from Oni Press!
Polly & the Pirates TM & © 2005 Ted Naifeh. Unless ottherwise specified, all other material © 2005 Oni Press, Inc.
Oni Press logo and icon are TM & © 2005 Oni Press, Inc. All rights reserved. Oni Press logo and icon artwork created by Dave Gibbons.

Creepy Courtney Collections
From Oni Press...